Skeeter

Skeeter

K. Smith

Houghton Mifflin Company
Boston   1989

Acknowledgments

I would like to thank the following people for reading the manuscript and giving me their support: my mother, Ruth Peeler; Helen Morris; Nick Lyons; and Mary Hunt. I would also like to thank my editor, Mary Lee Donovan, for her guidance and help. Finally, I wish to thank my former students in Grinnell, Iowa, who taught me about hunting.

Library of Congress Cataloging-in-Publication Data

Smith, K. (Kay)
  Skeeter / K. Smith.
    p. cm.
  Summary: The adventures of two young boys befriended by an old black man who is a legendary hunter.
  ISBN 0-395-49603-9
  [1. Friendship—Fiction. 2. Hunting—Fiction. 3. Afro-Americans—Fiction.] I. Title.
PZ7.S6524Sk   1989   88-37114
[Fic]—dc19   CIP
                      AC

Printed in the United States of America

P   10 9 8 7 6 5 4 3 2 1

To Glenn Leggett and David Jordan

One

"Some outdoorsmen!" Charles Ryder said. "Quail season opens, there's snow on the ground, and you two can't even crawl out of bed."

"Snow!" Joey exclaimed, tossing off the comforter. He hurried to the window, scraped off the frost, and stared in disbelief. A hunter's snow, clean and soft, powdered the farmyard and stubbled fields.

"I thought that would get you up."

"Tracking those birds will be a piece of cake!"

"You'd better get going. Steve has to be home by three."

"Three!"

"Duane wants him to help unload and install their new refrigerator. You can't stay out all day, either. I want that south pasture fence repaired by the time we get back from Memphis."

"All right."

"Have a nice day, son. Be careful and stay on our land. Remember to give Steve the message from his dad. I don't think he heard me."

1

"Sure, Dad. Bye."

Joey quickly pulled on his pants.

"Steve, those fields are going to be one big shooting match! Get up and look out the window!"

"Forget the window," Steve mumbled.

"If we don't hurry up, the sun will melt all the tracks." Joey lobbed a pillow at the covered hump. "Now move!"

Slowly Steve sat up. "Wish we had a dog."

"We won't need one on a day like this. Come on!"

Steve went to the window, hoping to share Joey's enthusiasm, but all he saw was snow bathed in early morning light. Below, the barnyard was silent and still save for the crow of White Lightning, the Ryders' rooster. Steve shuddered. He always found the dawn gray and gloomy, even ghostly, reminding him of the nearby country cemetery where lopsided slabs of gray Tennessee marble fought a losing battle with time.

"Let me at some food," Steve said. "Then I'll be fine. You know the only thing I love more than sleeping is hunting."

The boys finished breakfast and headed into the morning, confident the day belonged to them. They searched around brush for coveys of quail and scoured the acreage near the house. They found nothing. They looked for tracks in the snow, but saw nothing. The morning wore on, and the snow melted away beneath their feet. Hours passed. Discouraged, they stopped to eat. After lunch, they searched the far reaches of the property, but still success eluded them. By early afternoon they found themselves facing an unfamiliar thicket.

"Where are we?" Steve asked.

Joey shrugged.

"Great! We're lost!"

"No, we aren't," Joey insisted, afraid to admit his igno-
rance. "I think we're near Skeeter Hawkins's place."

"Skeeter Hawkins! I'm not staying here."

"Relax! He won't hurt us."

"Oh yeah? He blasted Rob and his friends with a double-
barreled shotgun."

"They set fire to his outhouse. Besides, he just fired into
the air to scare them. He didn't hit anybody."

"He could have. Besides, I distinctly remember your dad
telling us not to mess with Hawkins."

"Crossing his land is not 'messing' with him. He's just an
old man whose family is dead. He's alone and he wants to
keep it that way."

"That's not all there is to him, and you know it."

"No, I don't. Dad mentioned that Hawkins was known
for something years ago, but I wasn't paying attention."

"He was probably known for shooting people! Well, he's
not getting the chance to fire at me!"

"Now, wait a minute. We'd be stupid to retrace our
steps. The way I figure it, cutting through these woods will
be a short cut."

"A short cut to disaster, you mean!"

"Look, if Hawkins is even alive, he's ancient. He's probably too old to even lift a shotgun."

"I don't intend to find out. Your dad told us to stay on
your land, and my dad would have a fit!"

"Why, because Hawkins is black?"

"My dad doesn't like us being places where we don't

3

belong. Besides, this guy goes around shooting off shotguns, and he just might shoot us. Now, let's get out of here!"

"No," Joey said defiantly. He always hated to admit he was wrong, and preferred speed to safety. "That's silly. Let's cut through here, save time, and come out near our property line."

"Joey, I have to be home by three. If your figuring is wrong, we'll really be lost, and I can't spare the time. Neither can you. If that fence isn't fixed when your dad gets home, you won't be hunting for a year! And I distinctly remember him telling us when we got our .22s to stay off Hawkins's land."

"Then stay off!"

The boys stared at each other. Steve started to turn and leave, then hesitated. He had no idea where they were, and without Joey he might never get home.

"I'll protect you," Joey said teasing.

"I don't need protection. I am not scared!"

"Then quit acting like a chicken and follow me."

Joey headed briskly toward a clump of cedar. Steve followed reluctantly, loudly complaining, "This is the worst idea you've ever had, Joey, and you've had some pretty rotten ideas!"

Nothing looked familiar, and Joey knew they were lost. He was not even positive of which direction they were heading, but the prospect of meeting Skeeter Hawkins at the end of a shotgun was of no concern. Joey figured an encounter might be worth the telling, especially since he was confident of his ability to talk himself out of any predicament.

The boys continued to walk through the woods until they came upon a small clearing where a large brown rabbit sat munching grass. With an unspoken agreement between them, Joey nodded while Steve raised his shotgun and fired. Their renewed enthusiasm for the hunt began to dissipate as they stared down at the carcass.

"My mom told me not to bring home any more rabbits until we eat the ones we shot last year," said Steve.

"My mom won't do handstands when she sees it either."

"We might as well skin it and give it away."

"I don't want to skin just one rabbit!"

"I don't either, but we really shouldn't leave it."

"One time won't hurt. We've never left an animal before."

The boys stepped away from the rabbit.

"You boys! What's goin' on?" A deep raspy voice startled them.

The boys turned toward the voice and froze. A black man was staring at them with penetrating, angry eyes. He was huge and had a halo of white hair. A faded, quilted jacket covered his frayed khaki work clothes, and his feet were firmly planted on the ground in a worn pair of work shoes. Joey wondered if the old man was Skeeter Hawkins, but he had no idea what Hawkins looked like, so he simply assumed the worst and bit his lip. When neither boy answered, the old man called out again.

"You boys! This man's talkin' to you. What's goin' on?"

"We were out hunting," Joey replied in a squeaky voice, "and we shot a rabbit."

"You did?" the man said in a mocking tone. "Why, I thought you boys was settin' up a lemonade stand. I was

5

fixin' to buy me a glass. Boy!" The man's voice became menacing. "This land's mine! It's posted, and I don't recall sayin' you could hunt!"

The boys shook their heads stiffly.

"Now, what plans you got for that dead rabbit you was fixin' to leave?" The boys exchanged guilty looks for both knew the unwritten law of hunters: animals killed were animals used, not animals abandoned. But the old man's question made Joey think that maybe the stranger was more concerned about his stomach than their behavior, so he offered a bit too eagerly, "You can have the rabbit if you want it."

"Ain't you nice? Mighty white of you boys to offer me somethin' that's already mine. But I ain't leavin' it like you was fixin' to. Ain't I right?"

"Yes, sir," Joey mumbled.

"You boys know that's wrong."

While both boys were sorry, neither wanted a lecture. Steve whispered nervously to Joey, "Let's run!"

Joey started to agree, but paused the moment he realized that he did not know which way to escape. Then he had an idea. The old man would get them home. He took a deep breath, then asked, "Do you want this rabbit?"

"Yep. Bring it over here. My legs ain't what they used to be."

"Let him get it!" Steve hissed through clenched teeth. "He gives me the creeps. Let's get out of here!"

"Don't worry. He's going to get us out."

Steve responded with a contemptuous smirk that Joey ignored. Joey picked up the rabbit by the ears and said,

"Mister, can you tell us the shortest way to the Ryders' place? We were cutting across your land when we just happened to see the rabbit. We promise we won't trespass again."

"Follow me!" the old man commanded. Joey obeyed, but Steve crossed his arms and stood his ground.

"Steve, would you come on! He's showing us the fastest way out of here."

"That's what you think. How do you know what he's up to? He said his legs weren't too good, but he took off like a jack rabbit in a field fire. Being lost is bad enough. I have no intention of being led into a trap!"

"I can get us home, but he can save us time!"

"Why don't you just admit we're lost?"

A loud command from beyond the trees interrupted the boys. "Come on now!"

Steve glared at Joey. "I'm not taking any orders from him either!"

"Orders! Who's taking orders?"

"You are. 'Bring me that rabbit! Follow me!' You may be crazy. He's definitely nuts! But, I'm not crazy!"

"No, you're a deaf chicken! He said that his legs weren't what they used to be. He didn't say they weren't too good. But go ahead, backtrack if you want. I'm following him because he's older than the state of Tennessee, and I've got my shotgun!"

"We're lost, aren't we? Admit it! You don't even know the way out of here without tagging after him. You don't even know if that crazy man is Skeeter Hawkins!"

"Who do you think he is, O. J. Simpson? Stay here if you want, but I'm going!"

Steve waited until Joey vanished from sight. He looked around him, then seeing no choice, caught up with his friend. "I don't know what I'm going to tell my dad."

"Don't tell him anything! We go over to Mo Hunt's house, and he's black."

"That's different. We go to school with him."

"And he's a star football player. Your dad doesn't care who we hang around with as long as the person plays ball. Just tell your dad we found a retired tackle for the Saints out in the woods."

"Leave my dad out of this!"

"You brought him up!"

The argument stalled as the boys picked their way gingerly through a patch of dried briars. When Joey stopped to remove the brown stickers from his pants legs, he asked, "How come you're scared of him? He's big, but he doesn't appear to be dangerous."

"I just don't like the way he looks. You watch, Joey. Any funny business from him, and I just might bag something today!"

When they finally emerged into a large clearing, they were winded and surprised to see their guide rocking on the porch of a small unpainted house.

"Boy! That old man's fast!" Joey said as he stopped to catch his breath.

"He's really showing us the way, isn't he?" Steve said sarcastically.

"We probably head out back of the cabin. That's north."

"So what?"

"Come on in the house," the old man called out. "I got somethin' to show y'all."

"I'm not going!" Steve said.

"Suit yourself." Determined to show his courage, Joey strode across the clearing with the rabbit held out like a peace offering.

A shack, Steve thought. A typical shack like the ones he saw when he drove with his dad along the back country roads. Always the places seemed the same, peeling paint or no paint, cement block foundations, dogs and junk littering the yard, and smell. He heard the places always stunk to high heaven. Steve watched with growing irritation as Joey mounted the steps, spoke to the old man, and disappeared inside the house.

"Son, come on up," the man called again.

Steve tried to ignore the call, but he could not escape the old man's gaze.

"Ain't nothin' to frighten you, son. Got somethin' you want to see."

Steve bristled at the man calling him son, but he was increasingly uncomfortable standing alone, trying to ignore the invitation. Tentatively, he took his first steps toward the house. He noticed that no junk lay in his path. Still, he sniffed the air for stench. Nothing peculiar came to his nostrils. As he walked slowly toward the old man, dogs began to bark from under the sagging wooden porch. Steve tightened his grip on the shotgun.

"Hush up, you dogs!" the owner ordered, and there was silence.

Steve approached to within five feet of the steps, stopped, and swallowed nervously. The old man continued to stare at him with a smile that the boy could not return, and he was very relieved when Joey burst through the screen door.

"Steve! Get in here!" Joey said. "You won't believe this!" Then he vanished again inside the house.

Steve stepped on the porch and nodded as the old man held the screen door open for him. He entered a one-room cabin, sparsely furnished but immaculately clean. There were two multicolored rag rugs, an iron bed covered by a faded, pieced quilt, a wood burning stove, a small battered smoking table, and a kitchen area tucked in one corner. While Steve was startled by the lack of furniture, he saw nothing to arouse his excitement.

"Look up on the walls," Joey said.

Then he saw them — twenty of the most beautiful guns he had ever seen. Their stocks bore intricately carved designs and gleamed like the diamonds in Henderson's Jewelry Store window. Beautiful engravings covered the receivers. Steve had read enough sports magazines to know that he was staring at guns worth thousands of dollars, and the fact that the collection belonged to an obviously poor man only added to his amazement. He wondered but was too embarrassed to ask how the old man acquired such collector's items. He scanned the racks until he was drawn to a .30-30. He was saving his money for one but nothing he could purchase would ever equal the gun in that rack. "Isn't this a Winchester .94?" he asked.

The old man nodded. "Go ahead, son. Feel it if you want."

Steve ran his finger over the intricate pattern on the receiver and moved his hand slowly to the rifle's stock. The face of a large buck dominated a carved forest scene, and Steve counted the animal's points.

"Sixteen," the old man stated, as if reading Steve's mind.

The boy glanced at the man, then returned to examining the gunstock. He had heard of a hunter getting a sixteen-pointer, but a deer of such size was very unusual. Steve moved his face closer to examine the antlers and gasped. He could not believe what happened nor would he ever be able to explain it, but for a fleeting moment he was positive that the buck had returned his stare.

"Who carved these?" Joey asked as he stood before an old double barrel.

"I did," the man replied.

"Where did you learn how?"

The old man smiled and took a worn and pitted pipe from his pocket. "Teached myself."

"These are incredible!" Joey said. "Do you have any more?"

"Ain't them enough?"

"Sure! Oh, excuse me." The boy stepped toward the old man and held out his hand. "I'm Joey Ryder from up the road. We've been in the old Lewis place for ten years."

"Yep, I know."

"You must be Mr. Hawkins."

"Most folks call me Skeeter."

"My mom tells me not to call adults by their first name unless they say I can."

"Well, boy, I sayin' you better."

"This is Steve Foster. He lives in town."

Steve nodded awkwardly and pushed his hands farther into his jeans pockets. He was studying a beautiful .22.

"You two good friends?" Skeeter asked.

"Best friends," Joey corrected. "We're together so much that people get us confused."

"Oh?" Skeeter said as he filled his pipe from a Mason jar of tobacco.

"We're both five seven," Joey explained. "Same brown hair, hazel eyes, but you can tell me by my hair. It goes in all directions. Steve's just hangs straight like Robert Redford's."

"Believe me, tellin' you apart ain't no problem. That boy's got some meat on his bones."

"I know, I'm thin," Joey said, "but I'm not always going to be scrawny."

"You ain't? How do you know so much, boy?"

"Because my older brother used to be scrawny, and he filled out. He's a big college man now. Guess you remember my brother?"

"Guess I do."

"Sorry about that. My folks are visiting him today, and I would appreciate it if you didn't tell my dad about seeing us. He has a thing about staying on our land."

"Don't fret none, boy. Ain't seen yo' daddy since he brung yo' brother over to apologize. Don't git around much."

"Thanks. Anyway, I'm working out with weights, pumping iron." Joey demonstrated, his thin arms slicing the air.

"Don't go wearin' yo'self out, boy, pumping lead. Y'all sit down a spell. We have us a talk."

"We can't. We have to be home before three. I have to

fix a fence, and Steve has to help his dad move a refrigerator. Believe me, I'd rather stay here. But thanks for showing us your collection. They're really something!"

"They sure are," Steve said, continuing to stare at the guns.

Skeeter did not press or register any disappointment. Instead, he announced, "Before y'all go, we has time to clean ourselves a rabbit. Carry that carcass out here on the porch."

Skeeter walked out the door while Steve and Joey rolled their eyes. They did not understand why the three of them had to skin one rabbit. They knew any old man would be slow. Joey, however, picked up the rabbit. "I'll get us out of this," he said.

"You'd better," Steve said.

"Here, hand me that ole rabbit," Skeeter instructed, and he laid the animal on a crate covered with newspaper. "Stand back, so you won't git bloodied. Watch how I do this."

Before either boy could register completely what was happening, Skeeter was skinning the animal. "See how I made them cuts?" he said as he swiftly peeled the skin away from the flesh. "Here, boy, take that rabbit to the kitchen. Lay him in the sink," he said, handing the carcass to a startled Joey.

Skeeter wrapped up the remains in the newspaper and thrust the package at Steve. "Son, go bury this out in the garden patch behind the corral. You find a spade leanin' on the fence."

Steve dutifully carried the package to the garden. He hesitated before picking up the shovel, then began to dig. When he had finished the small hole, his disgust at the situation returned. "Taking orders!" he said out loud to a scarecrow

13

whose brown cotton shirt flapped in the breeze. "And he calls me son!" The scarecrow's dirty black hat nodded. "Son! What a laugh!"

When Steve returned to the cabin, Joey was sitting on the front steps stroking a big black cat. Skeeter was rocking in his oak chair.

"Say, Steve," Joey said. "This is A. Philip Randolph, the best mouser in the county."

"Yep, ole A. Philip Randolph can smell a mouse a mile away."

"Funny name," Steve said.

"Named after A. Philip Randolph, head of the Brotherhood of Sleepin' Car Porters. Big labor leader in his time. Stirred things up. Just like that cat; he keeps things stirred up 'round here. Jumps the dogs when they outta line, threatens the mice. Yep, couldn't run this place without him. So y'all been quail huntin'?"

"Yes, but we haven't even seen a quail today," Joey answered.

"Where's yo' dog?"

"We don't have one. You know," Joey said with an air of authority, "sometimes a dog can be more trouble than it's worth."

"Yep, it can."

"Joey, we've got to go home," Steve said.

"Say, Mr. Hawkins, can you tell us the fastest way to get to our place?"

"Mister Hawkins can't, but Skeeter can — on one condition."

"What's that?" Joey asked.

"Y'all git back here some time and talk to this ole man."

"Sure!" Joey answered without consulting Steve. "Will you tell us about the guns?"

"Maybe. Can't talk about all them guns at one sittin'. Git me winded."

"You've got yourself a deal," Joey said, never glancing at his companion.

Steve remained silent. The guns interested him. However, he did not want visiting Skeeter Hawkins to become a habit, and he knew well Joey's easy disregard of anything besides his own immediate interest.

"Now, if one of you boys will help me down them stairs, I'll set y'all out right. Times my knees git stiff headin' down."

Joey immediately offered Skeeter his arm. "Why don't you put a railing on these stairs?"

"Oh, don't get some things done."

The three walked across the clearing to a small opening next to a large cottonwood. Skeeter issued directions that would lead the boys out of his woods a quarter of a mile from the Ryders' property line. Steve started off. Joey followed. "Thanks again," he called out to Skeeter, waving. "I sure enjoyed it!"

Skeeter, alarmed at the boy's sloppiness with a loaded gun, yelled, "You welcome, but you gonna be dead. Turn 'round, boy, so you can see where you headin'."

Joey smiled and obeyed. The old man shook his head. Only when the silent woods had completely enveloped the teenagers did he turn and walk back across the clearing to his cabin muttering to himself, "Well, Lord, they's not what I expected, but they's finally come."

Two

One week passed and a second began. The boys did not return to visit Hawkins. Steve had filed away the encounter as a peculiar, if interesting, experience and forgotten about the man. But for Joey, who thought living in the country offered few diversions, visiting the old man with the gun collection was something different to do. There was no time, however, because the two were busy after school with the annual Future Farmers of America fruit sale. Each afternoon they loaded the Ryders' blue truck with cardboard cartons and drove the back country roads, making deliveries. Always looking for an opportunity to hunt, they brought along their shotguns, strapped securely to a gunrack in the rear window of the pickup's cab. The best-looking spots along the road were almost always posted or so fenced in that access was almost impossible. Occasionally they did find a spot and walked over it carefully, shotguns ready and nerves alert. But only once were they successful. Joey flushed a covey of eight quail from a clump of wild grape vines, and Steve downed one bird.

16

"Eight quail, and I get one!" Steve said. He kicked a patch of dried brown leaves and sent them crackling with his boot. "One quail! I should have stayed in the truck!"

"One's all Skeeter needs. Pick up that quail and let's go."

"Skeeter! Why do you want to go back there?"

"I want to see his guns again."

"Joey, you don't just keep going back to his house asking to see his guns."

"Why not? He told us to come and see him."

"He's just a lonely old man. We go again, and we'll be stuck. He'll expect us to come back and listen to him wheeze. Then he'll tell us about his cemetery plot and how everybody he knew died. That's what my great-grandmother does. I can't stand that death stuff. It gives me the creeps."

"If he starts wheezing, we'll leave. In the meantime, we're finished with our deliveries, and we don't have anything else to do unless you want to go to the Dairy Queen for the seventh time this week. Now come on!"

"All right, but I don't want to stay long. And he better not start that 'son' business again. I've already got a dad, and he isn't black!"

"Just shut up and get in the truck!"

Skeeter was rocking on the porch when the boys pulled into the clearing. He accepted their gift politely, but instead of simply taking the quail, he carefully examined it. Skeeter gave a detailed description of how and where Steve had made his shot, an account so accurate that both boys stared in amazement.

"How did you know how Steve was positioned?"

"Been 'round guns all my life. You boys aim to git where

17

the bird ain't gonna have all yo' lead in his backside?"

Steve nodded and reddened.

"Well then, boy, go git that L. C. Smith off the wall, that ole double barrel side-by-side on top of the first rack. We can have us a little practice. You can show me what you know. I can show you what you don't."

Joey disappeared inside the cabin almost before Skeeter had the words out of his mouth. Skeeter headed down to the clearing and turned around, expecting to find Steve behind him. Instead, he saw the boy combing his hair on the porch.

"Do combin' yo' hair make you a better shot?"

Steve smiled nervously. He had not joined in because he did not know what to say to Skeeter. After the command from the yard, he decided he had no choice but to pocket his comb and follow along.

Joey fired off a volley of questions as he bounded out of the cabin. "Say, why did you carve nuts all over this stock? Where did you get it? I've never seen one like this. Can I shoot first?"

"Boy, you some nut to come tap dancin' down them steps with a gun in yo' hand. What if that gun loaded? It would blow off yo' hair and we'd send you back to yo' mama lookin' like an egg."

Smiling, Joey stopped in front of Skeeter. "Now, why would you let us practice with a loaded gun?"

"Maybe 'cause I ain't worried 'bout you hittin' nothin'."

"Listen. You're looking at a number-one shot. Deadeye Ryder, they call me. Last year those doves just fell out of the trees when they heard me coming."

"Most likely somebody else shot 'em, you just picked 'em up," Skeeter said, warming to Joey's playfulness.

Steve laughed, then caught himself.

"Now, let's see if this gun fit. Hold it up to yo' shoulder." Joey obeyed. "Yep, it a bit too long, but it do for now. Boy, see that window in that shed over by the garden? That gonna be yo' target. I want you to walk 'bout ten feet, holdin' that gun like you walkin' in the field. When I go 'whoosh,' pivot and mount toward the window, pretendin' to shoot."

"One question. What's 'whoosh'?"

"That ole bird comin' outta the brush. Ain't a number-one hunter never heared no birds?"

Joey took four steps when Skeeter ordered, "Stop! Boy, quit stranglin' that gun! Son, you see him stranglin' that gun?"

Steve started to answer, then nodded. Skeeter was starting the "son" business again.

"What do you mean? Watch this!" Joey mounted his gun. "Now go 'whoosh,' because I'm ready."

"Boy, no bird gonna see you waitin' and decide to kill hisself flyin' in front of yo' gun. Don't never mount 'til you got a target. Now head on over there and stop."

Twice more Joey mounted to Skeeter's "whoosh."

"Boy, you look like you done been wired together. You need to move in one easy motion, like this." Skeeter demonstrated with an imaginary gun, his liquid torso a model of his words.

Joey mounted one more time. "I just shot me a covey of quail with three ducks thrown in!"

"Shoot, boy! The only bird you killed died laughin' at you." Skeeter started toward Joey, then called to Steve, "Come on, son. You listen to this, too."

Silently, Steve followed.

"Now, boy, you got the basics. You good at keepin' yo' eye on the target, and you good at pointin' out that target with yo' left hand as you bring that gun 'round, but like I done told you, the rest ain't together. Relax from yo' waist up. Keep them arms movin' until you fire. Move 'em, don't cock 'em."

"I thought I worked my hands together."

"Nope. Watch this." Skeeter demonstrated. "You movin' this right hand a second too late. You want that finger on that trigger when yo' brain tell you to fire, and that ole brain work the moment you git that gun lined up with the target. All good shotgunnin' men use their brains, but bein' good take lots of practice. Them ole birds smart. Ain't none of 'em gonna stand there hollerin' 'Shoot me! Shoot me, please!' "

"I know that!" Joey said. "I've been hunting for years."

"Humph! Then git yo' peach-fuzz self ready and try it agin."

Joey practiced five more times before Skeeter said it was Steve's turn.

Steve mounted three times for Skeeter, and the man was not impressed.

"You do lots of rifle shootin', son?"

"Yes," Steve answered awkwardly.

"Is that a rifle in yo' hand?"

"No."

"Then quit aimin' it like a rifle. Now when I go 'whoosh,' you gonna turn towards that target, watchin' it all the time, pointin' at it with yo' left hand bringin' that gun 'round. You ain't never gonna sight yo' gun. All right, try agin."

Steve repeated the exercise three more times while Skeeter stood, perplexed. Steve stopped each time and looked at him for an opinion, but Skeeter never responded. Finally he walked over to the boy.

"Still wrong. Let me follow through from the front to where that gun come back to yo' shoulder." Skeeter put his arms around Steve, who stiffened. The strong brown hands grasped the shotgun, and the teacher instructed, "All right, son, go slow now." Steve tried to obey, but he was frozen by the unwelcome familiarity of Skeeter. Steve's family, while close, was not physically demonstrative, and he would have been embarrassed by the embrace of any man, much less one who was black. However, Steve was learning something he valued. Taking a deep breath, he bit his lip and moved. "Hold it!" Skeeter ordered when Steve had the gun to his shoulder. The large encircling arms dropped and Skeeter stepped around to look closely at the way Steve positioned the gun. "Do it agin." Steve repeated his actions. "All right, son. I see it now." Steve relaxed and listened.

"The gun touch yo' cheek, not yo' shoulder first."

"My cheek?"

"Yes, got to git that hand with that eye first. Now, don't bang yo' cheek, just barely pat it like a girl do when she give you that first peck. Suppose you know all 'bout girls and kissin'?"

"Not likely," Steve replied.

"You gonna learn that just like you gonna learn this. Now, bring that gun back agin, son, and brush past yo' cheek first, keepin' yo' eyes on that target all the time."

Skeeter watched closely as Steve obeyed. "Now hold it," he said when Steve had the gun's butt against his shoulder. "Yo' gun a bit too high. Put that gun down and raise yo' right elbow."

"I feel like a chicken," Steve said.

"A chicken all you gonna hit 'less you git this right. Now, feel that hollow spot by yo' collarbone. That's where the gun go. Raise that gun agin. Bring it back. Just that tiny bit matter. Now, try agin, son. I'm gonna stand right here, and if I see yo' eyes lookin' at that bead, I'll spit in 'em."

Joey chuckled. Even Steve smiled. He knew that Skeeter was right. Steve could feel the difference in his swing, and he was excited about the improvement. He repeated the exercise five more times, then Skeeter called a halt.

"Now, you boys done wore me out. Come in and sit a spell."

"Could you give us a demonstration with a shotgun?"

"Boy, my firin' days over. My eyes ain't good."

"That doesn't matter. Wild Bill Hawkins once told me that you don't aim when you fire a shotgun. If you know how to mount the gun right, the shot will take care of the rest. You don't even need eyes."

"Boy, you sho' knows how to push yo' luck. How do you know I can see enough to raise that gun in the right direction? Might shoot you!"

"Will you do it? We've got some Mountain Dew cans in the truck, and I'll get my shotgun and shells."

"All right, but don't you boys go badgerin' me to do lots and don't ask me to fire no rifle 'cause this ole man is old!"

"How old is that anyway?" Joey asked.

"You a nosy one. Let's just say I got this century beat."

"Shoot, it's 1980 already! Are you sure you aren't a ghost?"

"Boy, go git that gun and hush up!" Joey ran to the truck and hurried back, handing his shotgun to Skeeter.

"How do you want Steve to do this?" Joey asked.

"What do you mean, boy?"

"Steve has the cans, so do you want us to whoosh or give some other signal? Do you want him to throw the cans one at a time, fast or slow, high, sort of high, low? I mean, we could —"

"Stop blabberin' for a start. You tirin' this ole man's ears. Son, just git over there and throw them cans any time, any way, while this jabberin' boy moves his backside."

"Are you ready?" Steve asked.

"Son, I done been ready for over eighty years."

Steve pitched the green cans high in the air, one right after the other. All three disappeared in a hail of shot.

Joey stared at Steve. "That was some wheeze!"

"You didn't do anything you told us to do," Steve said when he found his voice.

"Son, when you been on this ole earth as long as me, you git yo' own style. Y'all got to learn what to do startin' from the beginnin'. Now, you done wore this ole man plumb out. Here, boy, take this gun back to yo' truck. And, son, you hang the L. C. Smith back up while I git my rocker off the porch."

Joey hurried to the truck while Steve slowly carried the shotgun inside the cabin. He heard Skeeter dragging the old rocker across the floor, but he did not offer to help. Steve knew he should, but he was still uncomfortable with the familiarity and wished Skeeter would not call him son. Like a turtle who slowly peeks out at the world around him, Steve took one look beyond his own prejudices, then jerked back inside his protective shell. He really thought they should leave, but Steve did not want to be rude by forcing the issue. He examined the .30-30 again and noticed with relief that this time the buck did not return his stare.

Joey came in, and Steve hoped he would want to leave. Instead, Joey sat down on the floor next to Skeeter, and Steve saw no alternative but to do the same.

"How you boys comin' with the birds?"

"This year, not very good. We shot a grouse last week. So far no woodcock, and just two quail. We did all right during dove season. We want to go goose hunting, but Steve's dad has to take us, and he hasn't had time. Usually we hunt with him once a week, but he's been working a lot of overtime at the pipe plant."

"Sounds to me like you two out to shoot everything with wings. How old is you, anyhow?"

"Fifteen."

"And you drove out here by yo'selves?"

"My dad lets me drive out in the country. When I take Steve into town, he watches for the police. Lately we've been driving more because the F.F.A. fruit is stored in our barn, so I do the deliveries to the farms around here."

"I never had to worry 'bout no car when I was yo' age. Come to think of it, not many folks did."

"The pickup helps when we hunt. We always take our shotguns along. Today we saw these quail heading into the brush, so we stopped and flushed them out. That's how Steve got that one we brought you."

"Now, that's yo' trouble. Screechin' 'round the country makin' noise, jumpin' outta trucks. Y'all need a good dog and lots of time."

"We don't have a dog."

"I'll make a deal. Come over Saturday, and I let y'all take Abraham Lincoln."

"Abraham Lincoln?" Joey asked.

"The best hunting dog you ever likely to meet. He's gittin' old like me, but he needs to work out. Be real good to him, and he'll find them birds in no time."

"Was he one of those dogs barking under the porch the last time we were here?"

"Yep."

"Where is he now?"

"Him and his friend out by my pond. A. Philip Randolph run 'em out of the house this noon, and they ain't come back. That ole cat won't go near the water, so they go there to git some peace."

"You got any fish in that pond?"

"Joey!" Steve protested.

"Yep. They be real hungry by spring, too. But let's git back to huntin'. You want the dog?"

"Sure. We'll come, won't we, Steve?"

Suspicious, Steve remained quiet.

"Course, we ain't made our deal yet. You boys hunt, then stay to eat with an old man."

Steve wanted to object but did not know how. Before he could set any limits, he heard Joey ask, "Who cooks?"

"Y'all git the birds. I'll do the rest."

"Good, but could we come on Friday since tomorrow is Thanksgiving? We have Friday off from school."

"All right by me, and I guess Abraham Lincoln don't mind. Now, if you boys got some time, I got some time."

"We don't have much time," Steve said.

"Then what do you want to know in the time you got?"

"How did you get that collection?" Joey asked.

"Started with that ole double barrel side-by-side. When I was a kid, we had to hunt to eat. I didn't have no gun. Then one night me and my uncle come upon the sheriff shootin' a moonshiner for shortin' him. We hid and watched. Figured the moonshiner had a gun. He didn't need it no more, so once the sheriff took off, I snuck over and took it. Then I had to make it look like mine, and I carved it up. Was always whittlin' on something."

"What did you do about the moonshiner?"

"Nothin', boy. Just let him lie. No colored man turned in no white body 'less he wanted to hang. Figured the sheriff would find a way to git rid of him."

"You mean the sheriff was crooked?" Joey asked, wide-eyed.

"Crookeder 'n a barrel fulla snakes. Took that gun and left them parts as soon as I could. My papa and mama died when I's a little youngun. I just moved among my kinfolks like a mosquito at a picnic. That's how I got my nickname, Skeeter, 'cause I never lit long."

"Then where'd you go?"

"I come here. Had an aunt worked for the Dodges, the main family then in these parts. They lived in that big white house with the columns in town —"

"Doc Mager's house."

"Yep. Them days it was owned by the Colonel. Now the Colonel a huntin' man. So was his sons, the Judge and Mr. Manly Broom Dodge. One of their guns broke. I fixed it. That was the start. My auntie lived out back of the big house by the kennels. Hated field work, so I hung 'round the hounds. Soon I was workin' with 'em. Colonel seen my double barrel, asked me to carve him one. That was the start. Made me cash money. Still I didn't do lots 'til I marry Loretta. She had a son, Jerry. I raised him. Had a family, so I had to git serious 'bout money. Carved lots for rich men then. I'd carve, then buy myself, trade for better. Never sold that old gun. Remind me of who I is, where I come from, what I promised myself. Man needs to keep his promises, especially to hisself."

"What did you promise yourself? I promise things to people all the time, especially my parents. I don't usually do it, but I promise. I don't think I've ever promised anything to myself."

"You will. Got to find you some goals in life. Then you promise yo'self."

"So what did you promise?"

"Boy, you the only one with a tongue in yo' head?"

"Steve never talks much. He doesn't mind if I do."

27

Skeeter turned to Steve. "That true, son?"

"I talk. Joey just rattles and asks people questions he has no business asking."

"Funny! So what did you promise yourself, Skeeter?"

"Oh, don't know as you'd understand. Times has changed, but when I was young, bit older 'n you boys, I promised myself I'd git outta the fields, and I promised myself I'd never stoop."

"Stoop? You mean like this?" Joey asked hunching his shoulders.

"In a manner of speakin'. Now, what other gun interest you?"

Steve wanted to ask about the .30-30, but he held back. Joey immediately responded. "That L. C. Smith. That's an old gun. I bet it's worth a bundle."

"Maybe so. Maybe not. I won it off somebody."

"Doing what?"

"Shootin'. Worked for the Judge after the Colonel died. We lived out back in my auntie's place. Loretta work for the Dodges, too. Now the Judge had him two boys like his daddy 'cept Harrison almost growed 'fore Peter come along. Peter's mama died havin' him. He Jerry's age, so Loretta raise him up with Jerry. But Harrison a diff'rent time. He and the Judge always huntin'. One night we out with some of their friends from Birmingham. The men took to drinkin', and one of the friends brag he can outshoot anybody there. Bets his new .30-06. Harrison say I can beat him. Course the friend ain't thought of me 'cause I just along to work the dogs. But the Judge tells me to go ahead. I beat the man. Made him mad. He don't give me his new gun. Next mornin' he give me that ole L. C. Smith instead 'cause he don't want it no more."

"That wasn't right."

"I was a colored man. My winnin' 'ginst a white man was s'posed to be prize enough."

"Didn't you say anything?"

"See what I mean?" Steve said to Skeeter. "He never lets up with the questions. Joey, I've got to get home."

"All right, but let Skeeter answer."

"Boy, them times was long ago. Diff'rent rules for diff'rent folks. Son's right. It gittin' late, and yo' mamas likely to worry. Come back Friday, and Abraham Lincoln be waitin' to hunt."

As they drove into town, the boys discussed their lesson. Both were impressed by the man's apparent knowledge, but Steve was uneasy with their plans.

"How come you took him up on that dog without seeing it?"

"What was I supposed to do? Make him produce the dog before I agreed? He said the dog was good, and you said that Skeeter knew his stuff. Besides, a gamble is better than no dog at all."

"I know, but —"

"But what?"

"I don't want to keep going back over there."

"What?"

"Well, why should we?"

"Number one, the man improved our shooting. Number two, he's a terrific shot. Number three, he's funny. Number four, he wants us to come back. Number five, we will have more land to hunt, and his land is better. Any more questions?"

"Yeah," Steve said. "Do you get what he meant by not stooping?"

"I think so. You know adults are always telling us to stand up for ourselves, stand up for what we believe. I guess that's what Skeeter meant."

"So what's the big deal about that?"

"Skeeter's black."

"None of the blacks we know take anything off people. Joe Bradley flattened Henry Hodges one day in class when he thought Henry called him 'nigger.' "

"That's because things are different now, but you know Crazy Eddie?"

"Sure. He shuffles around town singing 'Twinkle, Twinkle, Little Star,' and we all bust a gut laughing."

"I think lots of blacks acted like Crazy Eddie years ago. They had to act dumb, at least that's what I've heard. I guess Skeeter never wanted to act that way."

"So? People can't help the way they're born."

"Crazy Eddie wasn't born that way. He's been that way since the Second World War."

"He got wounded?"

"No, he came back from the army, and some guys literally beat his brains out," Joey said. "They said he was acting smart just because he had been away, and they didn't like it. My dad told me years ago. All of the old-timers know. They just don't talk about those things anymore."

"He's that way just because he was acting smart?"

"That's what segregation was all about, keeping the blacks

in their place. You know, separate this, separate that, prejudice and all that stuff. Now do you see what Skeeter meant?"

"I guess. That's bad stuff about Crazy Eddie." Steve paused, then added, "Still, that dog better be good."

Three

The sun was barely up Friday when the boys knocked on Skeeter Hawkins's door. They were ready to hunt and anxious to see Abraham Lincoln. Skeeter had said the dog would be ready. When he opened the door without a dog beside him, Steve and Joey feared they had made a mistake.

"You boys up early for an ole man."

"We can't keep those quail waiting," Joey said.

"What bird told you he's gonna be out there waitin' on you?"

"We're ready to go! Where's Abraham Lincoln?"

"Well, boy, ole Abraham Lincoln ain't ready yet. Y'all best come inside and wait."

"How long?" Joey asked.

"Boy, you sit on some fire this mornin'?"

"No, why?"

"You actin' like somethin' singed yo' pants. You runnin' off in all directions and that mouth flappin', question, question, question."

Steve watched in amusement. Joey always hurried and did not like to be scolded.

"Them guns loaded?"

"Yes," Steve answered, "but the safety's on."

"There's quail all over the place!" Joey interjected.

"Well, there ain't no birds in this house, boy, so unload them guns and come inside."

Steve waited until the door closed behind Skeeter, then said, "This better be worth it, Joey. He's funny, and he knows his stuff, but I didn't drag myself out of bed to sit around talking."

"I know. Neither did I."

When the boys entered the house, they saw two dogs sprawled out asleep in front of the stove. A dirty white hound opened his eyes at their approach, but a mottled black-and-white dog with black ears never moved a muscle.

"Which one do you think is Abraham Lincoln?" Joey whispered.

"Has to be the white dog," Steve replied. "That other dog looks dead."

Joey leaned over to pet the white dog, but the animal bared his yellow teeth and growled. "Abraham Lincoln sure isn't friendly."

"That ain't Abraham Lincoln. That ole Orval Faubus."

"You mean *that's* Abraham Lincoln, your best hunting dog!" Steve said.

"Yep. Ole Abraham Lincoln's all tuckered out. Been out visitin' Franklin D. Roosevelt. He always visit with Franklin D. Roosevelt while he eat."

Steve shook his head. He had never wanted to get involved with Skeeter Hawkins in the first place. Now they were stuck with a half-dead hunting dog whose owner was undoubtedly crazy.

"Something the matter, son?"

"He keeps Franklin D. Roosevelt company?"

"Yep, that ole mule don't like to eat by hisself."

"Oh, Franklin D. Roosevelt's a mule."

"Yep. I done told Abraham Lincoln to take a nap 'fore he went out huntin', so he be rested."

"Do you think that dog can keep up with us?" Steve asked.

Skeeter walked over with a bowl of dog food.

"What about this dog?" Joey asked, hoping there was some way out of taking the sleeping hound. "Can't Orval Foobanks hunt?"

"Faubus, boy. Ain't you never heared of Orval Faubus? Course he was way 'fore yo' time."

"Nope, never heard of him."

"Well, he was the gov'nor of Arkansas. In the fifties. Tried to stop the integration of schools. Here, son, hand this to the dogs." Skeeter thrust the bowl at Steve. "Yep, ole Orval Faubus mean, white, and stubborn."

"The governor or the dog?" Steve asked nervously.

"Both, son. You just put down that dish and leave ole Orval Faubus alone. He ain't worth a plug at huntin', but he a good guard dog. Don't bother him 'til he decide if he like you."

"What if he decides he doesn't like me?" Steve asked.

"Then leave him alone, son, but put down the food. He won't bite now."

Steve quickly dropped the dish between the dogs, and Skeeter pushed Abraham Lincoln awake with his toe. The dog dragged himself to the bowl and began to eat, never pushing himself up on his four legs. Steve was astonished and tried to get Joey's attention, but his friend was pacing the floor examining the collection.

"What is this old rifle? It must weigh a ton."

"That's a European target rifle. Belonged to Mr. Manly Broom Dodge, the Judge's brother. He give it to me. It's a German Schuetzen."

"Bet I could hit a target with it."

"That gun's way too heavy for you. With a little muscle yo' friend might be able to aim it."

"Steve? I can handle anything he can! Shoot, last Sunday we were hitting cans out in the country with Steve's dad, and I hit better than Steve. Get that gun down, and I'll show you."

"Boy, you act like some policeman. Get this down! Put this here! Don't yo' mama teach you no manners? Besides, I thought you was here to hunt. Now you want to go target shootin'. You flighty as a sparrow."

"Can't we do both? The way that dog is eating, we're going to be here all morning."

"Boy, shootin' a rifle and shootin' a shotgun two different things."

"Don't you think I know that?"

"You may know that, boy, but what else you know beats me. Them ain't toys on that wall. Them are guns. Just like anythin' else, they can do right, they can do wrong. That depends on you. Man got to decide for hisself how and where he gonna walk in this life. To do that, he got to keep his mind on things! Yo' mind flies around like a gnat. Now, you here to hunt or shoot rifles?"

"Hunt," Joey said, determined not to show the scolding bothered him. "Say, how come you carved long lines on that Schuetzen? I thought you weren't supposed to mess with target rifles."

"Don't know that I 'mess' with no guns. Carved them lines to lighten that gun. Too heavy for Mr. Manly Broom Dodge. Now, that gun fit my friend, boy, but it don't fit you."

"How long did it take you to do that carving and then polish the stock?"

"Two years on and off."

"Two years! That's a long time!"

"Two minutes a long time to you, boy. You got to settle down if you want to be a good hunter and a good shot."

"I am a good shot, and if you don't think so, just get that dog ready, and I'll prove it."

"And who taught you to be such a good hunter?"

"Taught myself mostly," Joey boasted.

"Thought so."

"I also went out and watched a lot when I was little. Then Steve's dad started working with us, taking us hunting and practicing on targets. My dad hunts some, but not like Steve's. He spends more time with us than he does with his own friends."

"That true, son?"

"Yes," Steve agreed, checking his watch.

"Don't you think I know anything?" Joey continued.

"Didn't say that. Knowed you can shoot from the other day. Just wanted to know who teached you. Can watch a bird fly. Don't mean you gonna sprout wings."

"Well, I'm not as dumb as you think."

"Good."

"How was your Thanksgiving?" Joey asked, purposely changing the subject.

"Fine."

"Where did you go?"

"No place. That's why it be fine."

"Don't you like to go out, even on a holiday?"

"Don't like to go out, especially on a holiday."

"Don't you have any family around?" Joey asked.

"My wife's dead. So's my son. But my wife had a sister, Fanny Jackson, and she still here. She got a daughter, Shirley, and them two invite me. They always invite everybody needin' a place to go. I ain't needin' no place when I got right here. Too much noise and bother for me. I only go Christmas."

"Now what's wrong?" Steve asked in exasperation as he pointed to Abraham Lincoln asleep again on the floor.

"He digestin' his food. But since you so all-fired anxious, just mosey over to Abraham Lincoln. Let him git yo' scent, then go on out. He'll come when he git ready."

"You think that dog can catch up with us?" Steve asked.

"Just do like I say."

The boys obeyed, and Skeeter had the dog wake up and smell them. When the old man was satisfied, he walked the boys to the door.

"Head directly west by that ole magnolia next to Franklin D. Roosevelt 'til y'all git to open fields. No one hunt my land, so they'll be plenty of birds. Now, don't go shootin' in the woods."

"Why not?"

"Listen, boy, Abraham Lincoln very partic'lar about huntin'. You go gittin' flighty and shootin' trees, he gonna git nervous and think you hit him by mistake. Be back here 'round noon for lunch. I'll cook them birds."

"Noon! We can't be back by noon!"

"Why not, son? Has yo' limit by then. Ain't no other reason to stay out."

"The sun will go down, the moon will come up, we'll still be scouring those fields, and you expect us for lunch with our limit!"

"Git along now, boy, with yo' mouth. We see where y'all be at noon."

The boys picked up their shotguns and headed across the clearing. "Take good care of Abraham Lincoln!" Skeeter called.

Joey yelled back, "You'll see us before we see that dog!"

The boys disappeared into the woods. Skeeter sat in his rocker and spoke to Abraham Lincoln.

"Abraham Lincoln, you be careful with them boys. Don't confuse 'em 'cause they resemble. Same color hair, eyes, but they 'bout as much alike as a toad and a frog. That cute, likable boy don't got no patience. We doin' good if we make a shotgun man outta him. That other boy, the better-lookin' one, now he the rifleman. He strong, steady, quiet too, keepin' things to hisself. Right now he scared of us 'cause we strange to him. So you take yo' time. Now, come along. Time for an ole dog to work."

Skeeter shooed the dog out the door, then ordered, "Red-eye gravy!" The dog took off, and Skeeter watched as he ran past the magnolia. "Don't you be showin' off, Abraham Lincoln! Ain't no call to be wearin' yo'self out!"

While Skeeter and Abraham Lincoln were having their talk, the boys had hurried through the timberland trying to make up for lost time. Neither had bothered to look back for the dog. When they reached open land, they stopped to reload.

"We didn't ask Skeeter any commands in case that dog finds us this afternoon," Joey said.

"Who needs commands? That dog won't find us. He'll be snoring away the afternoon. Let's go!"

The boys headed off across open land looking for birds. The field was perfect. Low clumps of wild rose provided excellent cover and low-lying grass made walking easy. They had just reached the foot of a small hill when Steve grabbed Joey's arm and exclaimed, "Would you look at that!"

Joey looked up. Wide-eyed, he said, "It can't be possible!"

Abraham Lincoln sat at the top of the hill scratching his black ear with a look of total disgust at the boys' slowness. When the two hunters did not move, the dog barked, turned, and took off across the rim of the hill in a trot.

"Come on!" Steve said, and the boys hurried to catch up with the dog. Then Abraham Lincoln stopped short.

"Now what's that crazy dog doing?" Steve said.

"He's pointing, Steve! He's pointing!"

The boys raced to where Abraham Lincoln stood. The dog was facing a group of tiny, low-lying pine trees.

"What do we do now, Steve? Do you think he works to 'flush'?"

"Let me flush them."

Abraham Lincoln waited for Steve's first step, then attacked the brush, barking. A covey of twelve quail flew into the air. Joey raised his shotgun and fired. Soon Abraham Lincoln deposited two quail at Joey's feet. The boy was so surprised that he could not respond. Abraham Lincoln glanced, nonplused, at the boy and walked away.

"I sure wish we had those commands," Joey said.

"Joey, that dog doesn't need commands."

The boys spent the rest of the morning following Abraham Lincoln. The dog took his job in stride, setting, flushing, and retrieving birds, all accomplished with a total unconcern for interaction with the boys. Steve accepted the dog's independence. Joey, however, called out "Good boy. Good dog," whenever Abraham Lincoln approached with a kill, but Abraham Lincoln always dropped the quail at Joey's feet and trotted away before he could be petted. By eleven-thirty the boys had their limit and sat down to rest.

"And you thought we were wasting our time," Joey said.

"You were right. So was Skeeter," Steve admitted. "We're finished before noon, and Abraham Lincoln is the best hunting dog I've ever seen! I never knew a dog who could set and flush. I wonder what kind he is? He looks like a mongrel."

"I don't know what breed he is, but you can bet I'm going to find out from Skeeter!" Joey said.

"I wish my dad could see him."

"Well, bring him out here."

"Joey, you know my dad."

"Yeah, I know him well. He's a gun nut. He'd have already talked Skeeter into letting him fire half of that collection, and he'd love Abraham Lincoln!"

"Sure, he would. All I have to do is tell him, 'Dad, come on out in the country with us to see this great gun collection. It just happens to be in an old black guy's house, and you just have to sit around on the floor, let him call you son, and talk to him. Then he'll let you use his hunting dog.' "

"So?"

"He wouldn't come. Besides I'm not sure *we* should keep coming."

"Great. First you carp about wanting a hunting dog. Now you've got the best, and you don't want to take him out again."

"I didn't say that. I just don't know that we should keep coming back just to use the man's dog and see his guns."

"So what's wrong with that? Skeeter doesn't care. He likes us to come, and he said himself that the dog needs a workout. Besides, we talk to him, or at least I do. I think he's interesting. You just worry too much! Now, I'm going to find out about that dog. I'm going to have one just like Abraham Lincoln."

"How?"

"I'm going to find out from Skeeter where he got him

and how he trained him. Then I'm going to go out and buy one just like him and train him to be as good as Abraham Lincoln. Let's get back to Skeeter's. I'm starved!"

The boys stood up and looked around. Abraham Lincoln lay on the ground twenty feet away, totally uninterested in their presence.

"Joey, where are we?"

"I wasn't paying attention. This beats all! We get our limit and get lost!"

"That's got to be the first time you ever admitted being lost, Ryder."

"How should I know where we are? This isn't my land. The question is, how are we going to get back?" Joey did not even bother to listen for an answer as the solution dawned on both boys. They turned and looked at Abraham Lincoln. Cautiously, they approached him, feeling like beggars in search of a dime.

"You're the one who said he didn't need any commands, Foster. You get him home!"

"Home!" Steve said to Abraham Lincoln who responded by laying his head on his paws.

"Go home, boy!" Joey tried with no success.

Steve whistled, but Abraham Lincoln only rolled on his back and waved his legs in the air. "I don't know what else to do. Let's start off and see if we can recognize anything. The sun's still east and we came from the west."

As the boys walked away from Abraham Lincoln, the dog got up and barked. The boys turned to see Abraham Lincoln shake himself and head off in the opposite direction.

When they did not immediately follow, Abraham Lincoln stopped and barked again.

"See what I mean?" Steve said. "That dog doesn't need any commands."

"It would be nice to give him one command. I feel real stupid being led around by a dog."

Abraham Lincoln took the boys on a leisurely pace across the fields and back through the woods until they were in sight of Skeeter's cabin. Once they hit the clearing, the dog raced to the house. By the time the boys greeted Skeeter Hawkins at the door, Abraham Lincoln was fast asleep by the stove.

Joey questioned Skeeter about the dog, but the old man refused to answer until after lunch. He examined their birds, praising their shots on a few, and instructed them to clean several while he fixed the rest of the meal. After they finished their job, Steve gladly rested against a wall, while Joey tried to make friends with the dogs. Abraham Lincoln gave no response to a pat on his side, so Joey reached out and gingerly stroked Orval Faubus on the head.

"Good dog. Good Orval. Good old Orval Foobanks."

The dog snarled and grabbed his arm.

"Yeow!" Joey screamed. Steve laughed.

"That dog's mean!" Joey proclaimed after freeing his arm.

"He told you to leave the dog alone until the dog decides if he likes you," Steve said. "Guess he doesn't like you. Besides, his name is Faubus, not Foobanks."

"You're getting as bad as Skeeter," Joey said, clutching his arm. "Think that dog's insulted because I got his name wrong. The mutt probably doesn't even know his last name."

"Just you watch yo' tongue, boy. Don't go talkin' rude about Orval Faubus, or he git sulky and nip yo' other hand."

Joey gave Skeeter and Steve a scornful look, but even so he pushed his other hand up the sleeve of his hunting jacket.

Skeeter called the boys to the rickety table, and the three sat down to a lunch of fried potatoes, quail, biscuits, gravy, and coffee. Hungry from the morning's outing, the boys ate eagerly and quietly. When they finished, Steve and Joey helped clean up, and the three sat down before the Franklin stove.

"What breed of dog is Abraham Lincoln? He's colored like a mottled setter, but he's too small. He's a bit wiry and shaped like a spaniel, but he's too big. He's —"

"Boy, you askin' a question or answerin' one? Ole Abraham Lincoln hisself. He got a touch of everything, spaniel, setter, even the tinsiest bit of Lab."

"Where did you get him?"

"I didn't git him. I decide him."

"What do you mean?"

"I plan my dogs to git what I want."

"You mean you bred him?"

"Yep."

"Do you have any more like him?"

"Nope."

"Are you going to raise any more pups?"

"Nope."

"So I can't get one like him?"

"Nope."

"How did you get him that way? Give me some tips?"

"Tips?"

"You know, pointers. Tell me how to train a dog right. I'm going to get me a pup, and I'd like him to be as good as Abraham Lincoln. You're the only person who can tell me how."

"Just you go out and watch somebody. That's how you learned everything else made you so good."

"Can't you tell me anything? How do I get started?"

"First you need a good dog and plenty of time."

"I know where I can get a German shorthair."

"What's hair got to do with a good huntin' dog?"

"Everybody knows a German shorthair is the best."

"Oh everybody do, do they? That dog's hair teach him to be smart?" Skeeter lit his pipe and tossed the match into the stove.

"How long you gonna take to train this pup?"

"How long do I need?"

"If you has to ask, you ain't got the time to do it proper."

"So you won't help me? You won't tell me anything?"

"Can't, boy. Not worth the breath if I ain't seen the dog."

"I'll go get one!" Joey stood up.

"Sit down, boy. Sit down. You like a cat in a room full of rockin' chairs. Just relax. This ole man don't have no energy left to look at pups today. Plumb wore out cookin' and listenin' to yo' mouth goin' blam, blam, blam, like a machine gun."

"Can I bring over a pup tomorrow, so you can evaluate it while we hunt?"

"All right, boy."

"And can we take Abraham Lincoln out all day tomorrow and Sunday?"

"Y'all come over tomorrow, then Sunday after church, and Abraham Lincoln can go."

"What if we don't go to church?"

"It best to set y'all straight. Abraham Lincoln don't go huntin' on Sunday morning."

"I suppose he's a church-going dog?" Joey said.

"Not anymore, but he still a Baptist." Skeeter turned toward Steve. "Now, son, you mighty quiet as always. You want to ask any questions?"

"How do you get Abraham Lincoln home, or does he work to commands?"

"Don't need many commands with ole Abraham Lincoln. Still, can't let that dog take over. You git on his bad side, and he might lead you way past Birmingham. That's why I try to make that boy understand Abraham Lincoln bein' partic'lar. I don't want to git him nervous tellin' commands 'cause he might think he s'posed to git to work, but I tell y'all now how to git him home. The rest we can discuss tomorrow. Now listen up while I whisper the word." Skeeter leaned over, cupped his hands, and said softly, "Collard greens."

"Collard greens!" Joey said.

Abraham Lincoln's black ears shot up, and he bolted upright.

"See, boy, I done told you givin' the commands was gonna make him nervous. You done woke him up with yo' foolishness. Now you apologize to Abraham Lincoln."

Joey looked over at the dog. He felt silly, but he wanted

46

to hunt with him, so he obeyed. "I'm sorry, Abraham Lincoln. I won't wake you again."

"Relax, Abraham Lincoln. He just bein' careless," Skeeter said. The dog sprawled back on the bare floor. Skeeter looked at Steve. "Any more questions, son?"

Steve looked uneasily at the gunstock with the carved buck. "What's the story behind the .30-30?"

Skeeter took a long drag on his pipe. Then he stared steadily at Steve as if sizing him up, then nodded at Joey. Steve sensed that he had blundered into a private matter and was relieved when the old man finally said, "Son, time not right for that. You just wait. They'll come a time."

Uneasy with Skeeter's expectation of a continuing relationship, Steve stretched out on the floor to avoid further conversation. The morning had been successful. He had had a good time. As much as he hated to admit it to himself, the room was comforting. The warmth of the fire and the sound of Skeeter's rocker moving in measured time lulled Steve into a dreamy state, and he was soon sound asleep.

Joey could not relax. He had many more questions to ask Skeeter, but the man's eyes were almost closed.

"Can I take Abraham Lincoln for a walk?" he whispered.

"He tuckered out. But I can't git myself any rest with you flappin' all over the floor. Here, Abraham Lincoln," Skeeter said, pushing the dog awake with his toe. "This boy think you want to go walkin'."

The dog got up and went to the door with Joey in tow. The two headed down the road, the dog ten feet in front of the boy. The old man chuckled at Joey scurrying to catch the black-and-white blur. "Well, Orval Faubus, look like that dog's takin' that boy for a walk. Now don't you feel down. Someday it'll be yo' turn when that boy see Abraham Lincoln ain't his type."

Half an hour later the two walkers returned. Abraham Lincoln collapsed before the fire, and Joey looked totally dismayed.

"What's the matter, boy?" Skeeter asked as if he did not know.

"How come that dog ignores me? Most dogs like attention. Abraham Lincoln just goes on his way. I don't think he likes me."

"Boy, that dog don't need you. You not his type. A dog like ole Abraham Lincoln can't relax around flighty folks."

"I'm not his type! I just want to be his friend!"

"A dog like a man after his own type. Maybe you should ask Orval Faubus to step out."

"Orval Faubus! I'd never come back alive! He'd chew me up, spit me out, and claim he thought I was a bag of Gravy Train!"

"Hear that, Orval Faubus?" Skeeter said as he nudged the white dog with his toe. "This boy callin' you a killer."

Steve, roused by the conversation, opened his eyes. "What's going on?"

"I'm getting a complex from these dogs. They both hate me!"

"Some folks dog folks, that's all."

"I've always had a dog for a pet, and they've always loved me! I can name plenty of my friends' dogs who like me. It's just your dogs who hate me!"

"Maybe so, boy, maybe so. Gittin' home time for you two."

"Say, Skeeter, do you have any good grouse land?" Joey asked while he gathered his things.

"How come you need my land? Don't need no dogs for grouse."

"We do." Steve laughed. "We don't do well getting them. My dad said it was because we didn't know any good grouse land."

"Yo' daddy right, and I got some good land. But plenty time for grouse. Let's see first how y'all do with quail usin' Abraham Lincoln. If that ole dog decide on you, he'll show y'all some other good spots."

Steve nodded, relaxed. Skeeter expected them for the weekend, so he would appear. After all, he reasoned, he could always make an excuse later and not return.

"Goodbye, Orval Faubus!" Joey called out. The dog growled. "That dog's impossible! Everybody knows I'm good with dogs."

"Everybody don't know Orval Faubus," Skeeter answered. "See you tomorrow."

Four

"His name is Budweiser," Joey said. "Isn't he great? I just got him this morning. What do you think?"

"Son, you hold this dog on the way over here?"

"Yes."

"And what did he do?"

"Slept mostly."

"Figures. Boy, put this pup in the cabin and git on yo' way."

"Are you going to start training him while we're out? What are you going to do first?"

"Pin yo' lips together is what I'm doin' first. Quit botherin' these ole ears with questions. I look that pup over in peace and quiet. Ain't gonna take much time with that dog."

"Of course not. He's the best. He's a German shorthair."

"Son, when you ready to hunt, tell Abraham Lincoln 'Redeye gravy.' That means he s'posed to go to work. He stays with 'Chit'lins.' Think that's all you need for now. That ole dog is under the porch. You call him and git this blabby boy out to where the birds waitin' for him. Leave the dog choosin' to me."

"Okay, Skeeter."

Joey and Steve hunted for an hour until Joey could wait no longer for Skeeter's verdict. He assumed it would be positive, but he had a moment's unease when they returned, and Abraham Lincoln irritably roused the pup from his place by the fire. The shorthair dragged himself two feet before falling asleep again.

"That dog ain't got energy to walk, much less hunt!"

Joey suppressed an urge to cry, then sputtered, "But I paid plenty for him! He's a German shorthair!"

"Boy! I done told you havin' short hair ain't got nothin' to do with a good dog. If short hair be so great, they'd gone and shaved Lassie!"

Steve's laughter angered Joey. "It's not funny, Steve!"

"Yes, it is. You spent about two seconds picking out that dog. I told you not to hurry. Besides, Skeeter asked you yesterday what was so great about a dog having short hair. Now you know, it's not what's on the dog but what's in it that counts."

"So now you're the great dog selector. I don't remember your saying which one you thought was the best!"

"I didn't know. Skeeter's the one who knows."

"That's right. I wouldn't have done any better if I'd taken all morning because I don't know what to look for in a dog. But I know where there are some Labrador pups, and if you'll tell me what to look for, Skeeter, I'll have the prize of the litter here in half an hour. While we're at it, I'll see if I can take Budweiser back. If not, I'll sell him, but I'm having a great hunting dog, and I'm getting him today!"

"Can't tell you how to know the best pup, boy. My years with dogs tell me. But first off, the pup got to be wide awake, frisky, not like yo' Buddummer there, and it got to be curious and a bit stubborn. Y'all go git another pup, and I'll take me a look."

Within a half hour Joey and Steve returned with a small black pup who brought Skeeter to an immediate decision, "I said I take a look, and a look all I need with this pup. He sorrier than yo' sleepin' shorthair."

"Skeeter!"

"Don't 'Skeeter' me, boy. His head so small, he ain't got room for brains. Take him right back to his mama. She the only one gonna want him. Son, ain't you any help in this dog selectin'?"

"No, Skeeter. I'm just listening and learning."

"Well, you done wore me out lookin' at yo' pinheads and sleepin' shorthairs. Tomorrow you see if you can find a pup awake with a good head. Maybe you git yo'self started on a good huntin' dog."

"Tomorrow! Can't we finish today? Please!"

Skeeter responded with a determined frown. Knowing not to push his luck, Joey said, "You have my word, Skeeter. Tomorrow I'm going to bring you the best pup in the state of Tennessee!"

"Boy, you some kind of dreamer. You be doin' good to pick out the next to worstest one from a litter of two. Still, you boys show up tomorrow. We try agin."

Sunday afternoon Skeeter was throwing corn to his chickens when he heard the boys drive up. He put down the rusted red coffee tin and walked around to the front. Both boys waved, but Skeeter did not wave back because his attention was on a wobbly black plastic tent taped to the sides of the pickup bed. Abraham Lincoln and Orval Faubus were at the door, barking furiously. Skeeter ordered them quiet, but when they continued to whine and jump up, he suspected Joey had driven trouble into his yard.

"Skeeter," Steve said, "I bet you can't guess what Joey has in that tent."

"Don't take a contraption like that for one pup."

"No, but it does for twelve. He has the entire litter under that plastic and their—"

"Boy! What kind of dog man let you cart his young litter 'round the country?"

"No dog man did, Skeeter. He doesn't know. I talked his wife into letting me take them for a ride. She doesn't know a Labrador from a poodle, and I'm a smooth talker. She thinks I'm real sweet to think of the dogs."

"Humph! Any chance all twelve gonna git loose?"

"Not on your life, Skeeter."

"That true, son?"

"Skeeter, I take no responsibility for this. When Joey gets his head set on something, it's set."

"Listen, you two, I gave this construction a lot of thought. I put the black plastic over them, so they won't get spooked. They think it's night in there. But don't worry, I poked plenty of air holes for them. I couldn't tell the pick of the litter, so I just picked up the litter!" Before Skeeter could express his disgust, Joey's arms and head disappeared inside the tent. He reappeared holding a squirming black puppy. "What about this one?"

Skeeter examined the fur quickly and pronounced, "Coat wrong. Some hawk mistake him for a rat. He git scooped up 'fore he even git growed. Besides, his eyes set too close. He end up squinty-eyed."

"Skeeter, you sure are making this hard," Joey complained as he disappeared into the tent.

"You want yo'self a good huntin' dog?"

"Yes."

"Then don't go showin' me no rats!"

Steve laughed. Joey emerged with a second pup.

"How you tellin' them dogs apart since it night in yo' tent?"

"It's easy. They're nursing."

"Nursin'! Boy, you got the mama in there too?"

"Yes, but she's tied up. Now what about this dog?"

"Boy, when you give somethin' lots of thought, it got 'bout two seconds of yo' time." Skeeter quickly inspected the pup. "Put that pup down! We best finish this fast!"

Joey obeyed and the pup scampered around the truck within sight of Abraham Lincoln and Orval Faubus. They barked frantically.

"Oh no!" Skeeter exclaimed. "We'd better lock the door on them dogs of mine."

"What about that pup, Skeeter?" Joey asked.

"Too feisty," Skeeter answered quickly watching the pup with one eye while sizing up the situation with the other.

"You end up shootin' him to git some peace. He won't stay with nobody."

As Joey opened the plastic to replace the pup, the mother Labrador barked furiously and her cries electrified Skeeter's dogs. They bolted through the front door, answering the Labrador bark for bark as they jumped up against the side of the truck bed.

"Son!" Skeeter ordered. "Go git some leashes in the house, hangin' by the door! Then start tyin' up the—"

But before Skeeter could finish, the black Labrador shot through the plastic covering, followed by two of her pups. Abraham Lincoln and Orval Faubus gave chase, the three dogs streaking around the yard in a whirl of black and white. Skeeter and the boys stood stunned. When the dogs disappeared around the house, a third sound joined the cacophony—a chorus of shrieking, cackling chickens that jolted Skeeter and Steve into action. Steve ran into the house while Skeeter scurried toward the pen crying, "Lawdy, Lawdy! My hens!" Expecting Joey to be ahead of him, he turned to see the boy standing with a pup in his arms and watching the rest of the litter drop to the ground, one by one. "Boy!" Skeeter yelled. "Git yo' backside movin'!"

The old man scurried off around the corner of the cabin. The Labrador had turned the chicken pen into chaos. Orval Faubus and Abraham Lincoln remained outside the wire, barking and mirroring the Labrador's movements. Steve streaked past Skeeter and into the pen as the black dog backed a chicken against the fence.

"Save Mahalia Jackson, son! Save her!"

Steve ran toward the chicken, but he was too late. The Labrador had the hen in her mouth, and Steve had to pry open the strong jaws. He wrenched Mahalia Jackson free and raced with her to Skeeter. The Labrador cornered another hen, and Steve grabbed the dog's rope and pulled as Joey sailed through the gate.

"Boy, that dog git Eleanor Roosevelt, you be one dead white hunter! That's my best layin' hen!"

Joey dove for the first chicken he saw, which flew out of his reach. He turned and ran after a second, which escaped through the gate.

"Boy, you still don't know what you doin'! Save Eleanor Roosevelt!"

Joey stopped. Steve was straining to pull the Labrador from the pen and jerked his head toward the fence where a large white hen stood quivering against the wire.

"Is that Eleanor Roosevelt?" Joey asked with an impudence that further irritated Skeeter.

"Sho' ain't Mother Goose, boy!"

Joey took a deep breath, lunged successfully at the hen, and carried her to Skeeter. The old man cradled her gently and ordered Joey to help Steve leash his dogs and lock them inside the cabin. Once that was accomplished, Skeeter ordered them to collect the chickens that had escaped while he taped up the gate.

"How many chickens are there in all?" Joey asked.

"Fourteen chickens and one rooster. Eight's loose, and you'd better find all of 'em!"

Joey and Steve shooed chickens until their world became

one cackling bird after another. When they had finally secured the last chicken, they drove the truck to the far edge of the clearing and retied the Labrador securely in the bed of the pickup and taped up the large tear in the side of the tent. Skeeter watched their every move. When they thought they had finally returned the clearing to normal, he ordered them to collect the pups who were playfully scampering around the yard.

"Oh! I forgot all about them!" Joey said.

"That dog man ain't gonna forgit 'em when you show up without all his dogs. Yo' fast talkin' ain't gonna save you then!"

As the boys started their next chase, Steve angrily remarked to Joey, "You've pulled some stupid stunts, but this afternoon is an all-time low!"

"Yeah, well I don't recall your telling me it was stupid when you helped me put the dog in the truck."

"I told you I didn't think it would work!"

"But you didn't try to stop me!"

Steve shook his head in disgust. "Arguing with you is pointless. You always do what you want anyway!" Then he turned and began picking up pups.

Joey did not respond. He was angry—angry at himself, the dogs, Steve, and even Skeeter. Although he knew he was to blame, Joey still viewed the plan as basically a good idea that had gone wrong. He tried to vent his frustration by eagerly hunting down pups, but the exercise only added to his fatigue and irritation. Finally the boys found all but one black pup, which they gave up for lost, and went back to where Skeeter stood by the chicken coop. Skeeter stroked Mahalia Jackson's feathers trying to soothe her. Joey looked at the ruffled hen and offered to buy Skeeter another chicken.

"Can't git me nothin' I need, boy. Just take the trouble to git stuff in yo' head besides cotton balls! Mahalia Jackson be fine if you keep outta her way."

"Who is Mahalia Jackson? I know she's that hen, but everything else around here is named for someone."

"Mahalia Jackson a famous singer. Sung 'His Eye Is on the Sparrow.' "

"Well, I guess that's good. His eye was on the chicken today," Joey said in an effort at humor. Skeeter was not amused.

"Is there anything I can do, Skeeter?"

"Yes, boy! You can git yo'self in the pen and say you sorry to Joe Louis. That rooster don't like his chickens havin' nervous breakdowns. They can't lay good, and they give him trouble."

"Apologize to a chicken?" Joey asked, trying again to tease Skeeter out of his anger.

"No, boy, say you sorry to that rooster over there."

Joey slowly entered the pen and walked over to the sleek black rooster who flipped his red comb suspiciously.

"Joe Louis, I'm sorry about the dogs. I feel real bad about Mahalia Jackson. She looks a little winded, but I think she'll be all right." He walked back to Skeeter and Steve. "I've never apologized to a chicken before," he said. That was all it took.

"Corn meal mush!" Skeeter commanded.

Joe Louis attacked Joey, pecking at him through his denim

58

jeans. Soon the air was filled with the sound of Joey's yelps, the rooster's flapping wings, and laughter from Skeeter and Steve. Joey hopped around the pen shrieking, "Help, Skeeter! Call him off!" Joey tried shielding his legs, but that resulted only in sharp pecks to his hands. "Skeeter, stop him! Stop him!"

"Stop what?" Skeeter called, tears of laughter rolling down his cheeks. "Is that a chicken or a rooster after you, boy?"

"A rooster! A killer rooster! I won't call him a chicken again! Help! I promise!"

"You better not, boy. Farm boys callin' a rooster a chicken just doin' it to be ornery. You watch yo' mouth from now on."

"I will! Just call him off, Skeeter! Ouch! Help, he's hurting me!"

"Fat back!" Skeeter ordered, and Joe Louis stopped. Skeeter wiped his eyes with a broad white handkerchief and handed the cloth to Steve who took it and wiped his own. When he handed it back, he realized what he had done, but he felt all right. When he laughed with Skeeter, they seemed the same.

Joey left the pen in a huff. When Skeeter and Steve walked around the cabin to the front, they found Joey sitting on the porch steps with his head cradled in his hands.

"Now let's see about them pups," Skeeter said. By the time they had examined the third pup, Joey had forgotten his anger. The three looked closely at each dog, and Skeeter put every one of them aside commenting, "This all?"

"Don't tell me none of these will do?" Joey said.

"Just asked if these dogs here all you got?"

"All but one, Skeeter. We couldn't find the last pup, but we'll have to look again before we leave."

"That him over there?" Across the yard a black pup was determinedly chasing a bug in the dirt.

"Thank goodness. Now we've got all of them." Joey walked over and scooped up the pup. He held him up in the air to examine him. "Sure wouldn't have lost much with this one," he said as he handed the pup to Skeeter. "He's the ugliest one in the bunch."

Skeeter eyed the pup closely, and the dog eagerly licked his fingers. When the old man put him down, the black pup sniffed all around their feet. Joey saw the look of concentration on Skeeter's face, and said, "Please don't tell me that ugly thing is the start of the world's best hunting dog."

"This is a good dog. He stuck to his bug with all the commotion, mean he can stick to his business in the field with guns firin'. He good at stayin' with you, then hangin' in with the bird. He curious, so probably he smart. Bright-eyed, good-sized head, shiny coat. You make something good outta this dog if you do it right."

"But he's the sorriest-looking dog I've ever seen! Look at his ears! They're long and floppy, and they don't even match. He's got funny-looking legs, way too short for his body. I want a Labrador everyone notices. That dog probably won't even look like a decent Labrador when he grows up. And that face of his would stop a clock."

"Boy, you gonna hunt with this dog, or you gonna enter him in a beauty contest?"

"Hunt with him," Joey answered, knowing Skeeter had won his point. "But now what do I do?"

"Do? Do with what?"

"Do with the dog. Can I start training him?"

"Boy, when God passed out patience, he passed right over you. You was probably twitchin' so hard ole God mistook you for a June bug on its back. No, you ain't gonna start trainin' him yet. He ain't ready."

"Then, what do I do with him?"

"First, you name him. Second, take him home and let him git to know yo' ways. He need to git used to yo' twitchin', so it don't make him nervous. When the two of you git real thick, then we think 'bout trainin'."

"Well, at least I know what I'm going to name him."

"What's that?" Skeeter asked.

"Darth Vader."

"Where'd you git that silliness, boy?"

"It's from the *Star Wars* pictures."

"Boy, I watch the stars. I don't go shootin' 'em. That dog git laughed off the field by the other dogs if you go callin' him somethin' silly. You git serious now. Dogs don't like bein' peculiar. That's what you done to that sleepin' shorthair callin' him Buddummer."

"Budweiser, Skeeter. That's the name of a beer."

"Yes, and that dog of yours act like he drunk. Now like I done said, you git serious 'bout this namin'."

"What do you think he should call him, Skeeter?" Steve asked, knowing that Joey was defeated.

"Gonna call him somethin' to match his personality. This dog stood his ground with you makin' fun of him like he ain't nothin'. You don't think he can be the best, but this here dog's gonna show you. We gonna call him Jackie Robinson."

"Jackie Robinson! That's ancient history!" Joey stopped

61

himself when he saw Skeeter's insulted expression. He softened his voice and tried another tactic. "Why not name him after a modern black basketball or football player? How about Magic Johnson?"

"Um-umm," Skeeter replied shaking his head. "There ain't gonna be no magic in this here dog. He just gonna git good by hard work and natural talent. He gonna surprise you. You made fun of him because he ain't no beauty just like folks made fun of Jackie Robinson because he colored. But he showed baseball, he showed 'em all, and this dog gonna show you! Ain't you, Jackie?" The pup eagerly licked Skeeter's fingers.

"I don't believe this," Joey said watching the pup. "Dogs that know their last names. Roosters that kill on command, and now this pup can understand you."

"Some has it. Some don't."

"Well, you may have it, but one thing you're not is up-to-date! That dog is a black dog, so don't you go calling him colored. You know you're not supposed to call blacks colored anymore."

"Boy, when I was yo' age no colored boy called 'nother colored *black* 'less he wanted a fight. I growed up with *colored* or *Negro*. Negro too close to nigger to suit me. At my age I can say what I please! You can call me black, blue, whatever color suit you long as you don't call me white! Now take that mama dog home and come back. I got some brownies and lemonade my wife's sister brung me. We have us a dog-choosin' party."

As the boys drove out of the clearing, Steve said, "Skeeter is so funny. Jackie Robinson."

"I'm glad you think it's funny because I don't know what I'm going to call him at home."

"Call him Jackie."

"But what if my parents ask why I named him that?"

"They won't ask. If they do, just say you liked the name. When you say too much is when your parents get suspicious, and if you tell your dad, he'll tell mine."

"How long are we going to keep quiet about coming here? I don't like sneaking around. Why don't we just tell our dads and see what happens? Mine won't care."

"That's what you think," Steve said. "He won't even let you borrow a gun from me. What makes you think he won't mind you coming over here and borrowing Skeeter's dog, much less taking Skeeter's time? He has a real thing about you imposing on people. And remember how we met Skeeter in the first place? Your dad won't like it that we were hunting on Skeeter's property."

"Once he knows that Skeeter doesn't care, he won't care. I bet your dad won't mind either. He works with blacks at the plant."

"Yes, but he doesn't socialize with them."

"So who's socializing? Wouldn't bother me if we did, but I don't see how coming out here is going to make your dad angry."

"He doesn't like blacks, and I didn't tell him from the start. If I tell him now, he'll think I've been holding out on him, especially if he doesn't like it."

"So what are you going to do? Quit coming out here? That would be stupid. We've never had such good hunting, and Skeeter's a lot of fun."

Steve said nothing. He no longer knew the answer to Joey's question, and he did not want to think about it.

When they returned, the boys devoured Skeeter's refreshments while Jackie Robinson investigated the room. The older dogs were asleep, and the pup climbed over Orval Faubus's back. The white hound growled, and the pup scampered away. Next he pulled Abraham Lincoln's ear, and the dog opened his eyes. Joey picked up the pup while Steve called Abraham Lincoln. "Come here, boy. Come on." The hunting dog went to Steve and laid his head and legs across the boy's lap.

"Skeeter, would you look at that! I try to make friends with Abraham Lincoln, and he ignores me. Steve simply calls him, and he moves over like they're best friends! Skeeter, why does Abraham Lincoln like Steve and not me?"

"He's Abraham Lincoln's type. Ain't always askin' questions. 'You a dog? What kind of dog is you? How come you that kind of dog?' Abraham Lincoln needs a calm, steady, quiet person."

"Type! You and your types."

"I done told you, boy. You and Orval Faubus go out for a stroll. He yo' type, and he a good dog. Ain't no huntin' dog, but you ain't gonna need one after Jackie Robinson git growed."

"And I've told you, Skeeter! That dog hates me!"

"You ain't given him no time. You just sashay in here and take out Abraham Lincoln. Don't even pay no mind to Orval Faubus. Now you git him walkin', and he might grow on you."

Unwilling to concede defeat, Joey changed the subject.

"Your sister-in-law sure does make good brownies. Does she come out here often to look after you?"

"Nobody look after me. I boss myself."

"She brought these brownies over, so she must visit."

"Yep, she visit. Fanny and her daughter, Shirley, come over bringin' me stuff from the store. They wash my clothes, clean up a bit. They'd do more if I ask. I ain't askin'."

"Why not? I'd sure let my mother clean up my room if she would."

"Boy, just 'cause somebody do somethin' for you, don't mean you have to let 'em. I can cook, clean for myself. Don't like to be a bother to folks."

"Don't you ever leave here?" Steve asked.

"Not unless I has to."

"You mean you stay out here all the time?"

"As much as I can, son. Lived in town most of my life. Ain't nothin' I left there."

"Don't you miss things?" Joey asked.

"Like what, boy?"

"Movies, ball games."

"Never went to movies hardly. Ain't one to climb them stairs to the colored section. Used to see games later on the TV. The Judge used to come back to my place. We'd watch programs. Good shows then. *I Love Lucy* and *Yo' Hit Parade*. Ain't nothin' on now but noise and naked women."

"What's so bad about naked women?" Joey asked.

"Naked women ain't bad, I guess, boy, but at my age they ain't good neither!"

The boys laughed, then Steve asked, "Why don't you have a TV now?"

"Son, don't be stewin' 'bout me. You see nothin' in here 'cept a bit of this 'n' that. All I need now. The rest be bother."

"How come you moved out here?"

"Judge's brother, Mr. Manly Broom, left this place to me. Loretta gone, Mr. Manly Broom, too. I planned on comin' out here if the Judge go first. He did. They sold the big house. Nothin' left for me in town but mem'ries. Now y'all quit pesterin' me with yo' questions. Boy, let's see you take Orval Faubus for a walk."

"You're out to get me today, Skeeter. First you sic that killer rooster on me. Now you want me to get mauled by that dog. I tell you he hates me!"

"Nope. You just don't give him no time. Orval Faubus yo' type of dog. Take him out, 'stead of bein' jealous of them two, and maybe you learn 'bout yo'self."

"I'll try, but I'm warning you. If that excuse for a dog attacks me, I'll sue!" Joey walked gingerly over to Orval Faubus, who glared at him and growled. Having no better alternative, Joey growled back. Next he tried a friendly, "Want to go for a walk, Orval Faubus?" No response came from the body sprawled at Joey's feet. "See, I told you he didn't like me. I'm not his type."

"Humph! You some dog man. Always braggin' how good you is with dogs, and you can't even git that ole dog off the floor."

Joey knew Skeeter had him on the spot, so he turned back to the challenge resting comfortably on the wooden floor. He tried pleading with Orval Faubus, requesting politely that he accompany him on a walk, even lightly petting his head, all to no avail. "This mutt doesn't respond to my being nice."

"Well then?" Skeeter replied.

Joey assumed a position of command, took a deep breath, and announced, "Orval Faubus! Get up and move your backside out of this house! We're going for a walk! Let's go!" Joey slapped the dirty white haunch and took off before the dog could bite him. Surprisingly, Orval Faubus stood up and followed Joey out of the cabin. The moment they touched the yard, Orval Faubus raced toward the road, forcing Joey to run to keep up with him. Skeeter and Steve stood in the door chuckling at the comical race.

"Son, take them leashes we had on the dogs to the workroom. You'll see it out back if you follow that path next to the outhouse. Then come throw this stick to Abraham Lincoln. He don't need no exercise, but he like to frisk."

Steve was relieved when Skeeter gave him the tasks because he still did not feel comfortable alone with the man. Joey's presence guaranteed laughter. Without him, Steve grew uncomfortable. Skeeter's penetrating gaze, his seeming knowledge of what was on Steve's mind, his self-assured commands, were still too threatening to the boy.

When Steve entered the sagging workroom, he knew he had opened a door long closed. Cabinets and shelves covered with dust filled the room, and the silence of years hung in the air. Steve walked around, pulled open drawers, and recognized Skeeter's gunsmithing equipment. He gently picked up several tools and felt like he had opened a door onto himself. But he stopped, shut the drawers, and reminded himself that he belonged in town, far from an elderly black man who made him laugh. Steve knew that he should end the conflict within him by either telling his parents about his visits or by driving out of the clearing forever. But he could do neither, and the reason why frightened him almost as much as it prevented him from taking either road. He cared about Skeeter Hawkins. Unable to resolve the dilemma and uncomfortable with his feelings, Steve decided to make the obvious choice. He left the shed and ignored the problem. The next twenty minutes he spent out front, throwing to Abraham Lincoln. As the stick sailed through the air, he felt suspended in time, guiltless and peaceful. Somehow, being with the dog in the clearing was all right.

Skeeter pulled a chair to the door so he could watch. The sight of the boy and the dog brought into focus painful memories Skeeter had long suppressed, but the old man knew that he had found something he had been seeking.

When Joey and Orval Faubus reappeared, Steve and Abraham Lincoln had to get out of their way. Orval Faubus bounded up the stairs, and Joey followed ten feet behind. Joey collapsed on the porch. When he had caught his breath, he said, "You and your types! I don't know what you think that so-called dog and I have in common! He's impossible to take on a walk! He just runs around wild, barking at everything. One minute he's chasing flies, and the next he's off in the opposite direction smelling a log. He almost got killed when we hit the main road! He wasn't paying any attention when this truck came barreling along, and he darted right out in front of it!"

"Did he get lost?" Steve asked.

"One time. Hey, wait a minute," Joey said noticing the smiles on their faces. "Listen, I'm telling you, we're nothing alike. And he still hates me. Every time I got close to corral him, he snapped at me."

"He was just asking you a few questions," Skeeter said. Then he started laughing. "You and that dog really made the time gittin' in this house."

"About knocked us over," Steve added.

"Yep, run like a hound after rabbit." Skeeter laughed.

"I don't see what you think is so funny," Joey said irritably. Neither the old man nor Steve could stop laughing to answer him.

Five

Christmas approached. Red plastic swagging came out of musty storage boxes to decorate the main streets of town, and strings of multicolored lights appeared on the aged lampposts. Out in the countryside the old man waited, rocking away the time to the monotonous ticking of the clock. Christmas was a time of solitude for Skeeter Hawkins. He did not wait expectantly for Christmas Day to arrive, but for the season itself to vanish into the calendar of the new year. He wanted no memories of hand-hewn trees decorated with gingerbread men to disturb his peace.

The boys had seasonal jobs at the Big Bear Store which severely curtailed their hunting, so they visited Skeeter only twice in the two weeks before Christmas. Skeeter, however, was relieved, for their holiday chatter left him depressed. So caught up in the flurry of the season were the boys that they did not notice the old man's silence. When the two ceased a Christmas conversation, they started up on deer season, another subject of which Skeeter disapproved. He thought both boys were too green and untried, but he kept quiet as the two hunters bragged about imaginary triumphs in the field.

December 23 dawned cold and bleak, so Skeeter remained inside. He did not expect to see the boys again until after Christmas, so he was surprised when a vehicle pulled into the clearing. When he went to the door, Skeeter saw Joey taking a rifle out of his truck. Since the sky was overcast, threatening rain and possibly sleet, Skeeter assumed the boy had brought the rifle to show him and was totally unprepared for Joey's request.

"Hunt! This time of day with them clouds! You won't be able to see yo' way through the trees shortly, boy!"

"Oh, yes I will! I know exactly where I'm going. See, I found this perfect elm tree standing right next to the creek, and it has this one huge limb hanging right over the water with about a twenty-foot drop. I'll have excellent range once I'm on that limb for any deer unlucky enough to stop by for a drink."

"How you gonna reach this twenty-foot limb, boy? Fly?"

"No, there's this smaller oak with lots of climbing branches growing behind the elm. I'll climb up it and step over."

"Tell this ole man where stand this perfect tree."

"It's over that way," Joey said pointing in the general direction of the south timber. "I'll know it when I get there. I left some markings the last time. Don't worry, I'll find it."

"In this weather? Looks like rain, boy!"

"So? I'm going hunting, not on a nature walk. A little water won't bother me."

"Where's yo' friend? I don't like the idea of you goin' out by yo'self."

"He's working. I got off early. This is my only chance to hunt for four days."

"Well, you ain't gonna git nothin' on yo' only chance."

"Yes I will. I'm going to be the first person I know to get a deer. I even brought my skunk scent." Joey pulled a small bottle out of his coat pocket. "Want to smell, Skeeter?"

"Boy, put that mess away! Ain't no scent gonna cover up the smell of you. Maybe cover up yo' personal smell, but ain't nothin' gonna cover up the stink of this notion you got."

"Skeeter, please! Can I use your land? If you could see this elm, you'd know I've found the perfect spot."

"That's how you prepared yo'self for this hunt? Spotted yo'self a tree and bought yo'self a bottle of stink? Boy, it gonna rain, and that stuff ain't gonna be any help."

"Skeeter! Don't worry! I'll only be gone an hour or two."

"What kind of license you got, boy?"

"A juvenile."

"Ain't no growed person along with you."

"I can always say you were the nonhunting adult along."

"How I gonna be along when I ain't along, boy?"

"No game warden's out in your woods. The only trouble might be when I haul the deer home, and then I'll just take you with me."

"Just what I planned to do, boy. Drive around the country sayin' I been places I ain't been. You got peculiar ideas."

"Skeeter, can I go?"

"How many cartridges you shot outta that box?"

"None. I thought I would fire off a couple here, so you could watch and give me a few tips."

"There you go agin with yo' tips. You won't listen to what

72

I tell you. You ain't gonna go shootin' off in this clearin' 'cause I don't have it set up."

"You don't have to set up anything. I'll just shoot off a few at that cottonwood."

"Nope, ain't gonna shoot off any here, especially if you only shoot off two. Any real hunter know twenty bullets 'bout right to see how yo' rifle workin' with that partic'lar box."

"Twenty! That's too expensive for a few hours!"

"One bullet all it take to hit a deer. Course, you probably need six shots to git a mockin' bird flyin' two inches from yo' barrel. But that what I mean, boy. You don't listen to what I say, so why do you ask? Now let me see yo' rifle."

Joey handed Skeeter the gun he was carrying.

"You gonna use this .270 in the timber?"

"Yes. It will kill deer."

"This gun for long distances, open country."

"I know that!"

"Hold that gun up and aim toward the window."

Joey held the rifle in an off-firing position.

"Where'd you git this gun?"

"It's my dad's."

"Well, this .270 may fit yo' daddy, but it don't fit you."

"It will have to do because I don't have any other one I can use today. Besides, I can hit a deer with a .270. Now, can I use your timber?"

"No."

"Why?"

"Boy, sometimes yo' dumbness impress me. First, I don't like you huntin' by yo'self. Second, I don't like the idea of you climbin' up in a tree with a loaded rifle. You twitch so badly you liable to blow yo'self to kingdom come. Third, it bad out today, likely as not to git worse. You can't track in daylight, so how you gonna find yo' way out 'less you brought something in a bottle guaranteed to make you see in the dark. Fourth, that rifle all wrong. Fifth, that wrong rifle don't fit! Any more questions?"

"Yes. Can I go?"

"Um-umm, boy!" Skeeter muttered, shaking his head. "And what if I say no?"

"I'll go anyway. There's plenty of spots around. I don't have to use your land."

"Yo' mama and daddy know you out huntin'?"

"They're still at work, but they don't care. They trust me. Skeeter, you worry too much. Have I ever done anything stupid out hunting with Abraham Lincoln?"

"Boy, the dog and I talk, but he don't tell me everything! But since you so hardheaded, you can go for one reason and one reason only! At least I know where you is since yo' mama and daddy don't! Now, if you git hurt, I don't know what this ole man gonna do. You carryin' matches and a flashlight?"

"I've got a flashlight," Joey patted his side pocket.

"Matches?"

"Skeeter, I'm not going on a wiener roast. Why do I need matches?"

"In case you has trouble. Real dark out there at night. Sometimes folks need a fire for signals, warmin' up. But all right, boy. If you git in trouble, fire off three shots. Maybe these ole ears can hear you. And boy!" Skeeter took Joey firmly by his jacket collar, "You be careful! Don't be pullin' none of yo' stunts, takin' short cuts, bein' careless, gittin' twitchy. You hear me?"

"Yes, sir."

"And you be back right before it git pitch dark. Don't be trompin' through them woods at night."

"You sound like my mother." Joey smiled, but Skeeter was not amused.

"Boy, yo' mama need to teach you some manners. That mouth gonna git you whupped good one day!" Skeeter shook his head and went back inside without watching as Joey headed nonchalantly across the clearing.

Joey saw no reason to worry and dismissed Skeeter's warnings the moment he turned his back on the cabin. He ambled past the old weeping willow that marked the entrance to Skeeter's south timber and searched for his carved x's, greeting each discovery as proof of the wisdom of his plan. When he came to the creek's steep embankment, he again congratulated himself. Large gnarled tree roots pushed through the cracked earthen sides while below the shallow trickling stream wove its way around outcroppings of flat rocks. Joey looked for the elm. The long branch he sought stretched across the stream beckoning to him, and he hurried to the trunk of the tree where he poured on some of the skunk scent with a loud "Yuck!" Satisfied, he climbed up the oak, moved across to the waiting limb, and loaded his rifle. The first fifteen minutes passed quickly while he aimed at imaginary targets. When a fine mist began to fall, Joey pulled his rubber mackinaw tightly around him and he stretched out to wait, his long legs perched precariously on the limb, and his back against the trunk.

An hour passed and Joey began to get restless. He ate two Twix, then massaged his aching legs. When that did not stop the pain, he decided that if he exercised, he could last another hour. He did not want to go to the trouble of unloading his gun and climbing down, so he looked up into the elm and saw some excellent climbing branches on the far side of the tree. He rested his .270 across some small limbs, then pulled himself around the trunk and began to climb. He worked his way up carefully until he heard an animal noise in the creekbed below. Caution fled, and he began to descend with his usual disregard. He placed his full weight on a large, rotten limb, then heard a crunch. He tried to grab at branches as he fell, but he slammed against the bottom limb, barely missing his .270, and pitched into the creekbed below.

When Joey opened his eyes, he had no idea of where he was or what had happened. Slowly, painfully, his senses returned. He felt water beneath him, and his body throbbed. An awful odor made him gag. All he could think was that his friends had tossed him in a privy. He raised his head to vomit, but white hot pain shot through him so he simply rolled his head to one side. Finally, when he was able to lie still without retching, he began to take stock of his injuries, and memories of the accident slowly returned.

A sharp rock lay under his left ear, and Joey decided that that accounted for the dull throbbing in his head. His left arm was doubled up under his back. He tried pushing himself up with his right arm to free his left, but while he succeeded, the pain was so excruciating he had to lie back down in the freezing water. His teeth chattered, and Joey attempted to push himself up again. He felt for his left leg with his right hand and discovered that it lay at a ninety-degree angle to his body. Tears slid down his face when he realized that he was going nowhere. Soon he was sobbing.

When he had no tears left, Joey tried to think. Since he could not get out of the creek, he would have to signal Skeeter, and he remembered the last glimpse of his .270, hoping the rifle had fallen nearby. He reached into his mackinaw pocket for his flashlight, but found only crumbled metal and glass. To ward off mounting terror, Joey told himself that help would eventually arrive because Skeeter would worry and drive Joey's truck for help. All it would take was patient waiting in the dark. Joey breathed deeply, trying to keep his mind off his predicament. He tugged at his handkerchief to pull the Juicy Fruit from his jeans, and the loud rattle of his keys landing on a rock accompanied the freed cloth. Joey gave in to despair, but crying hurt too much while anger at his own carelessness made his stomach ache. He managed to push his head on a flat rock partially out of the water, then lay quietly, waiting for whatever happened. He searched for the moon overhead and remembered how as a child he had feared the dark. Then, mercifully, he passed out.

Skeeter had felt uneasy from the moment Joey left. He knew that the boy was destined for calamity. When Joey did not appear after dark, Skeeter waited another thirty minutes, then went to the pickup. He found the ignition empty and called Abraham Lincoln. The dog got the boy's scent and tracked Joey to the base of the elm. Frustrated, the animal stood on the bank and barked furiously.

Joey was deep in a dream where he, Steve, and Abraham Lincoln were out hunting, and Abraham Lincoln had just set off across the field barking. The dog barked and barked and barked. Slowly, Joey opened his eyes and thought he saw movement on the bank. Realizing that he was no longer dreaming, he called out as loudly as he could, "Abraham Lincoln! Here! I'm down here!" The dog slid down the bank, then splashed into the water. Joey welcomed the dog's licks across his tear-stained face.

"Abraham Lincoln, you're the best thing that's ever happened to me." He picked up his handkerchief and tried as best he could to wind the cloth around Abraham Lincoln's collar. He held the dog to him for a long time, patting the fur with his good hand, until he could order, "Collard greens, Abraham Lincoln! Collard greens! Go get Skeeter!" The dog barked and left.

The night again enfolded Joey. Mercifully, he drifted off again. He opened his eyes when he heard dogs barking off in the distance. A light was approaching, and Joey cried out, "Here, Skeeter! I'm down here!" Soon Skeeter stood on the top of the embankment holding a lantern.

"Skeeter!"

"Hold on, boy. I ain't no monkey like you, climbin' trees, jumpin' down creek banks. Don't want to break my neck gittin' to you. Gonna look for a good slopin' spot."

Joey followed the light with his eyes until it disappeared,

and he panicked, afraid that he had only dreamed of Skeeter's presence. Then he felt something nip his ankle, and a white dog was standing beside him.

"Orval Faubus," Joey muttered. "I'm lyin' here half dead, and you've come to finish me off."

The dog barked loudly, signaling the old man. Skeeter was carrying sticks and rags. As he approached, his face twisted in revulsion.

"Phew! What a stink! Don't know as I can stand this!"

"Skeeter, I'm so glad to see you."

"Well, boy, I ain't hoppin' up and down to see you lyin' there. Had better things to do than drag my old bones out this time of year. And I sure smelled better things! Might just keel over myself standin' here. Done faced many tough things in my life. Ain't gonna be happy to see St. Peter havin' to say I been done in by a bottle full of stink!"

"Skeeter, how'd you get here?"

"Ole Franklin D. Roosevelt brung me. By any chance, you got yo' truck keys with you?"

"Yes."

"Thought so. Thought you might plan on drivin' an imaginary truck with them keys in yo' pocket. Now let's take a look. For once, you don't seem to be twitchin'." Skeeter held the lantern over Joey and moved the light slowly up and down. "Lawdy, you a mess! This water'll freeze up soon, but I sho' hate to move you." He got down and looked closely at the broken leg. "Got a clean break. That's good. Now, git ready, boy, 'cause I got to git you to where I can move you, and it gonna hurt." Joey heard cloth tear, and a sharp, lacerating pain shot through him. "Oh God, help me!"

"God ain't gonna help you, boy, 'cause he can't stand the smell! Now we 'bout done."

The pain dulled, and Joey realized that Skeeter had bound his leg with rags around a branch.

"Now, we gonna git you over yonder on that dry bank. What can you move, boy?"

"I think my right arm and leg are all right."

"Then use 'em. Here, I'll git you sittin' up."

Skeeter knelt down and pulled Joey upright. "Now see this big stick here? Pull yo'self up as far as you can on the stick 'til I can help you. I can't git you all by myself. Don't have the strength."

Joey grabbed the stick with his right hand, tried moving his good side, so he could stand up, but the pressure on his left leg was unbearable. He gave up, crying, "I can't! I can't!"

"Then you has to sit in this creek and freeze while I git help. That leg'll be that much harder to pull outta ice."

"No! Please don't leave me, Skeeter!"

"I got to. The only question's where, here in this water or over there on the bank where I can make a fire?"

"Over on the bank," Joey gasped.

"Then git yo'self up. Help yo'self 'til this ole man can help you. I can't lift you, boy!"

Joey grabbed the stick, pulled up once, and quit. "I can't!"

"You can't! I hear you say you can't do somethin', boy! Why, to hear tell it, there ain't nothin' you can't do! You can hunt, shoot, trap, track, kill deer! And there ain't nothin' you need to learn! But now maybe you see you need to learn one thing — respect! That's yo' problem. You ain't got no respect for the land! No respect for the animals! No respect for the gun! You just tramp this earth like you king, stompin' so hard you ain't got to look, listen, or learn! You git yo'self some respect and maybe you'll finally learn to listen! Then maybe you'll learn! Now, boy, you gonna listen to me!"

"But it hurts!" Joey sobbed.

"It's supposed to hurt! Hurtin' is when you learn, boy! Hurtin' is what teach you to survive in this world! You hurtin' now, boy. You hurtin' enough to learn how dumb you is 'cause you ain't nothin' but one, big, mouthy know-it-all!"

Joey nodded, sobbing.

Skeeter thrust out the stick again. Joey pulled forward on his right hip, then inched his right leg toward his body and tried to pull himself up. He screamed when the pressure began on his left leg, but he continued pushing until he felt Skeeter's long arm under his own. Together they got him to where he could stand on his right foot. Joey's face was wet from crying, but he made no sound as the two slowly made their way to the bank. Skeeter put down the lantern and helped Joey slide down to the dry sand, then tied another cloth around Joey's head.

"Now, boy, you rest here. I build you a fire then go for help. Hand me them truck keys."

"Oh, Skeeter," Joey said. "They're in the creek. I pulled them out of my pocket by mistake and forgot to put them back."

Skeeter shook his head. "Boy, right now I'd like to bang yo' good side with this whuppin' stick! Think this ole man's Tarzan! Was them keys right beside yo' sickly self out in the creek?"

"They should be. Skeeter, I'm sorry."

"You sho' is sorry, boy, but not the way you think!" Skeeter went back to the creekbed muttering under his breath. When he returned and held out the keys in front of Joey, the boy asked, "Can I have my rifle, just in case?"

Skeeter shook his head. "Boy, you half dead and still stupid. No, you can't have no rifle. How you know it not dirty from fallin'? Then you pull the trigger, the gun go 'blam' in yo' face."

"I didn't realize it was dirty."

"Well, it is. I found it on the ground, buried in a pile of leaves. It goin' with me."

Joey watched as the old man moved around in the darkness, building a fire. Everything about him looked so comforting. The old, frayed quilted jacket, the faded bib overalls, the unprotected bald head, the large fingers carefully putting pieces of wood one on top of the other, all had grown so familiar and so very necessary. "Skeeter, I'm scared." Tears of pain, fear, and embarrassment rolled down his cheeks, and he began to cry. Skeeter looked over at the boy, and his anger left. The old man lit the small fire, laying more sticks in a pile by Joey's hand, then he put his arm around the boy. Joey gratefully wept against Skeeter's shoulder.

"Now, boy. Nothin gonna git you. You already done all the damage you can. Besides, nothin' in these woods want a puny rascal like you. Ole Skeeter gonna see you git outta here. Let's see that ole mouthy, smart-alecky smile."

Joey sniffed, but he could not stop the flow of tears. "I'm scared to be alone."

"You ain't gonna be alone. Orval Faubus gonna stay here

and protect you. I done told you he a number-one watchdog. You gonna be glad you took that ole dog for a walk."

"But he hates me!"

"Oh, hush up, boy! Ole Orval Faubus don't hate you."

"But he won't mind me."

"He will if you listen good. Now here yo' commands. To make Orval Faubus attack, you say 'pot liquor.' To call him off you say 'hog maw salad.'"

"Hog maw salad? I think I'm going to be sick again."

"Boy, there you go gittin' mouthy. See, you ain't dead yet as long as you can sass. Now, them commands in yo' brain?"

"Yes."

"Tell me quietly."

"Attack is 'pot liquor,' and 'hog maw salad' will call him off."

"That right. To send him home use 'collard greens,' same as Abraham Lincoln. Now don't be sendin' Orval Faubus off no place but home, then only if it necessary, 'cause he ain't a good tracker like Abraham Lincoln. We has us enough trouble without havin' one lost dog. Speakin' of dogs, we best get them rounded up, so this ole man can go git yo' mama and daddy."

Skeeter patted Joey on the back then called the dogs who were busy investigating the creek. He ordered Orval Faubus to sit next to Joey, and he left with Abraham Lincoln. The sounds of Joey's muffled crying followed them, but Skeeter did not turn around until he found the spot where he was to climb the embankment. Orval Faubus sat illuminated in the flickering fire. Joey's good arm was wrapped around his back, and the boy was crying into the dog's white hair. For a fleeting instant Skeeter thought he had slipped back in time to another boy, another place, but shaking his head, he came to himself and started up the incline.

Skeeter drove Joey's truck to the Ryder's farm and notified the boy's worried parents. Charles Ryder telephoned the rescue squad to meet them at the old man's place, and the three drove back to wait in the clearing. No one asked why Joey was on Skeeter's land. Faye Rider was too upset to do anything except have Skeeter describe the accident and Joey's injuries repeatedly. Charles Ryder, however, suspected that there was more to his son's relationship with Skeeter Hawkins than a one-time hunting trip.

When the rescue ambulance arrived, Skeeter refused to accompany the men to the creek. Instead, he startled the group by instructing them to follow Abraham Lincoln. Then he retreated to his rocker and waited until the dogs announced Joey's rescue. He watched from the porch as the crew and family emerged from the woods carrying Joey on a stretcher, and the old man returned the boy's feeble wave. He remained outside until Joey disappeared into the white ambulance, then, nodding to the Ryders, Skeeter went back inside his house.

Six

The accident shattered the wall of secrecy the boys had erected around the friendship, and Skeeter Hawkins awaited the outcome. He knew without being told that the boys had never informed their parents of the hours passed with him. He knew because he had spent his days as a black man in a white world, and he could read the boys' every expression as easily as he could tell the seasons by glancing at the trees.

Boys had been a constant in Skeeter's life. Judge Dodge's older son, Harrison, and his friends were the first ones to dog Skeeter's footsteps and grow to manhood wearing his instruction as a badge of honor, but they were the sons of wealthy men. Skeeter was a status symbol to them, and they returned with their sons to the master as naturally as they used the greens at the country club. But Skeeter had not limited his talents to the rich. As his local reputation grew, boys unknown to the front door of the mansion had come around back to satisfy their curiosity about the Judge's sharpshooting hired man. All who came were given one chance. Few measured up. Skeeter recognized that, while he might be a leader, he could not take his followers past the color barrier they penetrated so freely in reverse, so he drew his own boundaries around excellence, discipline, and attention to detail. Aside from Jerry and the Dodge circle, the only boys to meet his exacting standards were the ones like Steve, and Skeeter had recognized the boy the moment he saw him hesitating on the side of the clearing. Steve's kind always hung back, venturing slowly toward Skeeter, gradually shedding their prejudice as they absorbed the talent and integrity of the man. There had not been many. Skeeter needed only one hand to count the boys of mutual respect.

Skeeter knew that Steve was close to his father because of the frequency with which Duane Foster's name came up in conversations. But it was Joey, not Steve, who talked affectionately about the man while Steve looked uncomfortable. Skeeter had lived with prejudice in all its forms throughout his lifetime, and he could pick it up as easily as Abraham Lincoln could track a scent. Laws had changed, so times had changed, but Skeeter knew that in some families prejudice was still passed from one generation to the next like a family heirloom. Skeeter knew that Steve would have to make his own decision about returning, and that decision would depend on how much he cared for Hawkins. The boy would have to face his father, and Skeeter knew that the man could exact a very high price for disobedience. However, Skeeter thought he knew Foster's type. The man was a hunter. He would ask around about Skeeter, evaluate his skill and reputation, then decide how he felt about his son's continued relationship with a black man. If white skin meant more to Foster than anything, Skeeter realized he might never see Steve again. However, it had been Skeeter's experience that prejudiced whites could always cross the color line when they wanted something.

Joey was another matter. Skeeter knew that the boy would chase after him as playfully as a kitten batting a string. The friendly, open boy reflected his family, people easy to like but hard to respect, for while they gave easily, they gave with little cost to themselves. Skeeter knew their type well. The Ryders were people of the sidelines, never persecuting blacks themselves, but never crossing the color line unless or until it was necessary, then acting as if it had never existed. So Skeeter was not surprised when Joey's parents arrived on his doorstep two days after the accident with a basket of food for him and bones for the dogs. He accepted their gifts and offers of help with the polite indifference he reserved for well-meaning whites. He did not protest when Charles Ryder added a railing to the steps, and he allowed Faye Ryder to take him to the Oaks Cemetery where he laid handmade wreaths on Loretta's and Jerry's graves. During the drive Faye Ryder kept up a constant flow of conversation which reminded Skeeter of Joey, but she never mentioned Steve, and the question of his return loomed in Skeeter's mind. While he loved Joey, the boy was not sufficient for his needs. Only Steve possessed the inner strength and direction necessary to sustain a relationship with an elderly man who was beginning to give of himself again.

Two days after Christmas a car pulled into the clearing, and Skeeter Hawkins had his answer. He greeted Steve cheerfully at the door.

"Come on in here, son. How come you ain't home enjoyin' yo' holiday?"

"I can't stay long." Steve paused, then added as if to apologize, "This has been my first chance to get over. We had company for Christmas."

"That's all right, son. Come when you can. I don't have no call on yo' time."

"How was your Christmas?"

"Noisy. Half the town at Fanny's. Still, I enjoyed myself."

"I got my license."

"Noticed you drove out here by yo'self. How's it feel bein' sixteen?"

"About the same."

"How is the sassy-mouthed boy?"

"Better. I told him I hope his skull fracture knocked some sense into him. I told him not to go. He said you tried to talk him out of it."

"Didn't do no good."

"Joey never listens to anybody. He was really out of his head after they set his bones. He thought we were out hunting, and he would call Abraham Lincoln. Then he would yell for Orval Faubus not to finish him off. Mrs. Ryder phoned me, and I went to the hospital. I explained about the dogs. Joey's dad said he thought you were crazy when you told them to follow a dog to get Joey, but now he tells everyone about Abraham Lincoln."

Skeeter patted the dog's head. "Now, Abraham Lincoln, don't let all this talk go to yo' head."

"Joey wants you to come see him. I'll drive you over if you want to go."

"You tell that boy I need a rest from his mouth. Done traveled 'nough gittin' him outta that creek and tellin' his folks. I see him later."

"Joey and I got this for you." Steve dug into his jacket pocket and pulled out a small present wrapped in bright red paper. "Joey had it, so we didn't get it to you for Christmas."

"You boys shouldn't be spendin' yo' money on this ole man," he said as he slowly unwrapped the gift. "Uh-umm, a new pipe. I need this. Look here, Abraham Lincoln, Orval Faubus, look what them boys brung me. I have me a mind to try it out right now."

Steve called Abraham Lincoln over. The dog settled down happily, and Steve petted him with long, deliberate strokes.

"You got something on yo' mind, son?"

Startled, Steve looked up. "You always know what I'm thinking. My dad's birthday is in two weeks, and I wondered if you would help me with his present? I bought the stuff I need to load shotgun shells, but my mom won't let me do it by myself. A friend let his son do it alone, and he double-loaded a shell by mistake."

"That ended up a mess," Skeeter said.

"Yes. The gun blew up in the field, just splayed back like a flower. The man's hand and arm are really bad." Steve paused while he scratched Abraham Lincoln under the neck, then continued without looking at Skeeter. "Mom said that since Dad can't help me if it's a surprise, you'll have to."

"When do you want to come?"

"Is Saturday all right? I finish my job at Big Bear on Friday."

"Fine. You tell that boy he best send Jackie Robinson over here while he laid up. Ole Abraham Lincoln and Orval Faubus teach him to start actin' like a real dog. Ole A. Philip Randolph can teach him about cats."

"Where is that cat? I haven't seen him in weeks."

"Probably under the house. Don't like it inside. The dogs git on his nerves. That ole cat always come and go, mostly go. One time he off three weeks 'fore he drag hisself back."

"Speaking of dragging home, I'd better go."

"Good to see you, son. I git ready for Saturday, and thanks agin for the pipe."

"You're welcome, Skeeter. Oh, I almost forgot," Steve said as he pulled a rumpled card from his jeans. "We got this for you. It's messed up because I sat on it."

Sentiment always embarrassed him, so Steve hurried out the door while Skeeter opened the envelope. He glanced at the card and noted the signatures. "Thank you. Son, Boy." Smiling gently, he stepped out on the porch. Holding up the card he called out to Steve. "How come you changed yo' mind, Son?"

Steve started to ask what Skeeter meant, but he dropped the pretense. Skeeter had known all along how he felt about being called "son." "You said that a man's got to decide how he's going to walk in this life. Guess I just took a step."

Skeeter was pleased that Steve had returned, but he guessed

that the boy's father had not yet given his blessing to the friendship. When Steve returned on Saturday, however, Skeeter learned that Duane Foster had done exactly as he had imagined. When Steve entered the cabin, he was happy and relaxed, wasting no time in announcing, "Fred Mc-Crimmon said to say hello."

Skeeter said nothing. He remembered McCrimmon as a bristle-haired boy who was always trying to best someone.

"He's my dad's supervisor at the plant."

"And yo' daddy talked to him about me?"

"Yes."

"Well?" Skeeter said, lighting his pipe.

"Mr. McCrimmon couldn't believe you loaned us your dog. He told my dad that we should grab anything you were willing to let go of, but he couldn't get over your letting us use Abraham Lincoln. Guess that wasn't very nice of him, but that's the way he put it."

"Don't surprise me none. Sounds like McCrimmon. He always had lots to say when he was a youngun, mostly wrong things. What else did he say?"

"He said you were" — Steve paused in embarrassment — "funny about the way you did things."

"Funny ha-ha or funny peculiar?"

"Peculiar. Once when he was a kid, he said, he had his dad's .22 without permission, and he broke something on it. You fixed it for nothing, but when he was older you wouldn't do any work for him, regardless of how much he offered. He said you could have made a lot off gunsmithing."

"That all?"

"No, he mentioned that .22 up there." Steve looked up

at the gun hanging behind Skeeter's head. The dark walnut stock and forearm gleamed. Steve seldom looked at the gun because he could not hide his longing for the rifle that made his own Winchester look ugly by comparison. "He said your son was the best shot in the county. Nobody could beat him, and Mr. McCrimmon and his friends used to meet your son and the Judge's son out in the Dodge's timber and go squirrel hunting. Peter Dodge always carried a black walnut .22, a Winchester M52, and no one but your son could touch it. The stock was carved with a flying squirrel and the initial *P*. It made them all angry because they wanted it so bad. Mr. McCrimmon says he can still see that flying squirrel today. That's the gun, isn't it?"

"Yep. But it belonged to my son, and P stands for Pickens, Jerry Pickens, not Peter Dodge. I told you Jerry was Loretta's boy, but I raised him."

"So why was Peter Dodge carrying the gun?"

"Back in the late forties no colored boy s'posed to have such a fine gun. All right for Peter Dodge, a rich white boy, to be carryin' it. McCrimmon and his kind never question Peter, but Jerry havin' it woulda been diff'rent."

"Even if they knew you carved it for him?"

"Just him havin' it woulda made them mad. They'd figure out some way to git it from him. Didn't want my boy gittin' hurt over a gun. Didn't want the gun stole."

"You couldn't replace a gun like that if someone took it."

"Can't replace a man's pride either, but Loretta said I took that from Jerry by makin' Peter carry the gun when they hunted with white boys. Said even if Jerry lost the gun, didn't matter; she wanted him to have somethin' he could be proud of. And Loretta more trustin' 'n me. She raised Peter when his mama died and thought Jerry's bein' with Peter would protect him, but I'd seen too often what happened when white folks didn't like somethin'. Didn't want to put Peter in a bad spot."

"Bad spot?"

"Havin' to choose between Jerry and the way things was. Since they was raised together, nobody thought nothin' of them two always bein' together, but Jerry could never act like he as good as Peter. Carryin' a fancy gun around whites woulda meant Jerry gittin' outta his place. Nobody could have that. Them boys woulda turned on Jerry, beat him up, and pick a time when Peter around to see it. Peter woulda wanted to defend Jerry. But if he did, people say he questionin' the way things was. Nobody did that in them days. Peter probably woulda defended Jerry. I just didn't see any sense in testin' him. Too dangerous for Jerry. Them boys coulda beat him senseless."

"Is that like what happened to Crazy Eddie?"

Skeeter took a long drag on his pipe. "Somebody been talkin' to you about the old days?"

"Not really. Joey told me. Did Crazy Eddie question segregation?"

"The only thing Ed Barnes did was wear his army uniform once too often. Had him medals. Folks proud of him. But he held his head a bit too high, talked a bit too much. Some men got drunk one night and decided to teach him a lesson."

"Anything happen to the men that did it?"

"Sheriff ain't gonna arrest his own deputy and the men hangin' out on his office porch."

"You mean —"

"Son, Ed Barnes only one of many. I don't much like thinkin' about 'em."

"Were you ever threatened?"

"Nope. I figured out real early the one way I gonna survive was to make folks need me. Sheriffs always used me to track. I'd go out at night, go places scared them. Never lost anybody that needed bringin' in, but didn't always find the innocent colored boy they's blamin' somethin' on. One way to help."

"Why didn't you leave?"

"Didn't have no place to go. Never had no real family 'til I come here. The Dodges gave me a place. Maybe it not at the big table, but I had a place. Didn't see no point headin' north. Couldn't hunt, fish, breathe, in a city. These parts all I knew. The Judge, Harrison, Peter, all like my own family."

"Where is Harrison Dodge now?"

"Alabama. Married more money 'n he had. But he good to me still. Good to me then too, but not like Peter. Peter like my real son, not because he raised with Jerry, neither. Harrison knowed he was white. Knowed I wasn't. He never crossed them lines. But Peter was born not seein' folks diff'rent. He coulda really made Jerry his 'boy.' 'Stead, them like twins. Went to separate schools, separate churches. Otherwise, we couldn't keep 'em apart. Loretta told 'em they gonna have to hoe diff'rent rows in life. They knowed it, just didn't want to turn away yet. Never lived to say good-bye across the color line, though."

"What happened to them?"

"Ever heared of the Korean War, son?"

"I guess. I think *M*A*S*H* is supposed to be then."

"Jerry and Peter signed up for it. They say they not ready for college. Wanted excitement, so off they goes. Loretta turned out right sayin' folks gonna make them go separate ways someday. Couldn't make 'em in life, so did in death; Peter buried in the white cemetery, Jerry restin' at the Oaks. Guess they got back together up in Heaven."

Steve continued to stare at the .22.

"Now I got that gun. Don't got my boy."

Steve did not know what to say. Skeeter read his silence and continued, "Back to yo' daddy's boss. McCrimmon don't know lots. I made money off repairin' guns. But I made it from the Dodges' friends, men who could pay me what my time worth. 'Round here if I started fixin' this, fixin' that, folks expect me to fix anythin' for nothin'. Besides, my real money come from my carvin', and repairs took time away from my carvin' time."

"How did Jerry get to be such a good shot?"

"First he had the right temper, quiet, steady, like you. Started him out on BBs, then an old .22. He practice on everythin', tin cans, hand-drawn targets, the Judge's regulation targets. Jerry almost shot in his sleep. That's what it take, Son."

"I practice, but I don't practice that much. We don't have a place."

95

"Tell you what. You ask yo' daddy if he mind you settin' up a target range out here. Lots of stuff packed away in my shed. It's old and dirty. You boys clean it up, and we'll set us up a good range out front. You has to bring the ammunition. Soon we be loadin' and reloadin', so it won't cost much. But I ain't lettin' you fool with guns 'less yo' folks know and say it all right. If they agree, I agree, both you and that sassy-mouthed Boy."

"Oh, they'll agree. Joey's dad doesn't care as long as we aren't bothering you."

"Ain't no bother, Son."

"My dad will think it's great. He's tried to help me, but he doesn't have the time. I want to be a first-rate shot, and Mr. McCrimmon told him you were the best teacher there is."

"Time's somethin' I got plenty of. But how come you want to be such a good shot? Person needs a reason pushin' him to be the best."

"I want to be really good at something. I hate school. I can't talk to people like Joey can, but I'm good with my hands. I like to be outdoors, and I know I can be a good rifleman if I work hard. Then, who knows? The army has places for good riflemen, and there are competitions around."

"I understand, Son. Now we wait 'til that sassy-mouthed boy git his twitchin' self here to help. You and me git it all planned, then go ahead and start strippin' down guns, work on aimin' and loadin' shells. When that boy gits hisself back, he can do some shotgunnin' while you work on rifles. When you git tired, you can trade off. Y'all learn to be good on both kinds of guns. But you can only be the best on one. Now when you want to start?"

"I'll be here tomorrow afternoon, Skeeter. And thanks. Any message for Mr. McCrimmon?"

"Nope."

"You don't like him, do you?"

"Nope. Still, ain't good to hold grudges, especially since I's s'posed to be such a good teacher for you. Just say hello for me and tell him I's still funny."

Seven

Steve came almost daily. Together they planned the shooting range, uncovered the rest of Skeeter's collection, which lay buried beneath a trap door in the shed, and stripped and rebuilt two guns. They were alike, the old man and the boy. Neither made idle conversation. Each saw the need for perfection, and both were changing in each other's presence.

Steve was now completely at ease with Skeeter. His father's permission had been a blessing, freeing him from the tension that had wrapped him in a cocoon. He emerged like a butterfly, comfortable and free. Skeeter welcomed the new honesty, for now he could totally give of himself. One day he caught sight of himself in a mirror. His shoulders still sloped, lines still etched his face, but the man who returned his gaze had life in his eyes. Skeeter realized then that what he had found alone in the timber had been rest, not peace. Peace had come when he returned to what he knew best.

Initially the two seldom missed Joey. They needed quiet

to perfect Steve's aim and to study carving techniques. Once they had covered the basics, however, they were anxious for Joey's return. They missed his bantering and the laughter his antics provoked. Skeeter also came to realize that he needed Joey almost as much as he needed Steve, but for a different reason. The likable, blabby-mouthed boy had brought joy back into Skeeter's life, and he yearned to laugh again.

One February afternoon a car drove up, and Skeeter heard a loud whistle from the yard. When he went to the door, he saw Joey waving a crutch at him.

"I'm back and I'm ready!" Joey called.

"Ready for what, Boy? Fallin' outta 'nother tree?"

"No, you've got yourself a number-one hunter!"

"Couldn't no doctor put a cast on yo' mouth?"

"Don't need one, Skeeter. Now, just watch me hop up these steps. I'm almost back to my old self."

"Well, that ain't so good. I's hopin' you git back to yo' new self!"

Joey got up the steps, and Skeeter fastened his hand on the boy's shoulder.

"Dad said he fixed the railing. I guess something good came out of my accident."

"Yep, but that the only good thing. I bet yo' fall ain't knocked no sense into you."

"Probably not. Thank you for what you did, Skeeter. If you said that I couldn't hunt that day, I would have gone anyway. But I guess you knew that."

"Yep. One of these days, you gonna listen to this ole man. Course I probably be dead when that happen. Now git inside this house. Some dogs gonna be real glad to see you."

"I can hardly wait to see Jackie Robinson. Steve says he's already acting like a champion hunting dog."

"Git in there, Boy, and see for yo'self."

"Can I take him home with me, or do you think he ought to stay here with you?"

"Take him home. Time you started pullin' yo' load."

Joey hobbled through the door and picked up Jackie Robinson. Convinced that the two were again friends, he turned back to Skeeter.

"Listen, Skeeter —"

"There you go, Boy. One minute in this house and already you orderin' me to 'Listen, Skeeter'!"

"Now, come on. I'm serious. We're serious, aren't we, Steve? We've had a long talk with our dads. Actually the whole thing was Steve's dad's idea. He's talked to a lot of people about you. Most are surprised to hear that you're still alive."

"There you go insultin' yo' elders."

"Anyway, he said we should learn all we can from you while there's still time." Skeeter started to protest, but Joey continued. "Now, don't go getting all hot thinking we're ready to shovel you under —"

"Joey!" Steve protested. "Quit talking to him about dying."

"Don't fret none, Son. It don't bother me. Rather talk about it than do it."

"That's not what I mean anyway. As I was saying, Steve's dad says the two of us don't have much time left."

"Boy, y'all young."

"We know, but Mr. Foster says that pretty soon we're going to be getting steady jobs, not just these pickup things. And then there's women. I think about them a lot now, especially when I watch some of those red hot movies. Shoot, I may even get around to asking one out."

"One of them red hots from the movies?"

"No, Skeeter! You know what I mean. But right now we need to have our minds on learning from you, and I've been thinking —"

"That be something new, Boy."

"Come on, Skeeter. Steve and I have been talking. If we get real good at all of this, we probably could open up a gun shop. Maybe we could also run a game preserve. What do you think?"

"Possible. But don't go gittin' yo' plans ahead of yo' skill."

"Steve's dad thinks that your letting us set up a target range is the best thing we could have for our practice."

"The best thing you could have, Boy, is a closed mouth to listen to me. That possible?"

"Yes, Skeeter. He says for us to do exactly what you tell us, without arguing, since you know more about guns and hunting than anybody we'll ever meet. Nobody can figure out why you're fooling with us. You're supposed to be a bit strange."

"Peculiar," Skeeter said.

"Right. Anyway, Steve's dad said that as long as you've taken a shine to us, we might as well make the most of it. We won't get a chance like this every day."

"How you gonna make the most outta me? Gonna ask me question, question, question?"

"Only necessary questions. And while we're out here, we aren't going to do things only for ourselves."

"You ain't? Then, who you gonna do it for, the dogs?"

"Nope. My dad said that you probably could use some help. You've got plenty of land and probably some repairs. He thinks we should help you, and we agree. So you want something done, you've got us. Now, what do you want done? I could fix you some fishing poles, repair some old ones. I could cut that brush behind the house. I like to chop weeds and listen to music. Or I could take down all these gun racks, clean them up, and check them. Or —"

"Boy, give me some time to think. Right now I needs some rest from yo' mouth. 'Sides, them things all things you like to do. Won't learn nothin' from 'em."

"Who needs to learn? Now that's a necessary question. We just want to help you. You know, give you something in return."

"Can't think of anything right off to do for me. Can think of somethin' I want you to do for Fanny. Teach you some patience at the same time."

"Skeeter, patience I've got. Lying in that bed took lots of patience."

"Then, this won't be hard for you. And you gonna listen to me, remember? One of these days I want you to chop down a small white oak tree. Save some of it for yo'self. Cut the rest into logs. Then split them logs into halves and quarters, then into eighths and sixteenths. When you done that, you can trim them into even splits. I show you how."

"What for?"

"Fanny a good basket maker. She ain't made one in a long time, though. Ole man Winslow died. He use to make her the splits. She can make you a basket."

"A basket! Why should she make a basket? If you want a basket, I'll go buy you one at K Mart."

"Nope. You want to help, you help Fanny. Teach you about creatin' somethin' 'stead of just goin' 'round, blam, blam, blam, tearin' up and killin'."

"And what's that about saving something for me? What am I going to do with white oak?"

"You gonna chop it into pieces and carve them pieces."

"Carve! I'll cut my hands to ribbons. I can't even cut soap in art class."

"That 'cause you hurry. We gonna git you slowed down. Course it prob'ly take this whole forest of trees 'fore you git it right. But we start simple. You chop yo' pieces, then find one got a turtle in it."

"Turtles aren't in trees."

"They is if the wood's right. You look at that oak, find yo'self a piece with a turtle hidden in it. Then you gonna let that ole turtle out by carvin' it free."

"Why can't I do gun stocks like Steve's going to when he gets good?"

"'Cause first you gotta work on slowin' down."

"Baskets and turtles. I'm going to feel like I'm back in kindergarten. But I'm going to do it your way because I'm going to be the best rifleman in Tennessee!"

"There you go, boy, already settin' yo' sights wrong. What if I say you can't be the best with a rifle?"

"I won't like it, but I'll listen, and I won't twitch!"

"That's where you wrong agin. You can't help that twitch, so we gonna put it to use. You can be the number-one shotgun man in the state. Son here's the rifleman 'cause he's slow, deliberate."

"Then what about the target range? I don't want to build something I can't use."

"Who's sayin' you can't use it? Both of you can learn on a rifle and a shotgun. Out in the field, you need both. But, Boy, you ain't gonna have the patience for rifles. Shotgunnin's more to yo' talent. You git to move with it."

"Steve says you have an old trap out in the shed. Can I use that?"

"Sometimes, but we gonna use a hand trap most of the time. It better practice. That ole trap just throw 'em one way. Used it for the Dodge's trap shootin'."

"Trap shooting is something I've never done. Maybe I can get real good and win a bunch of medals."

"Boy, you just learn how to shoot first. Then we see."

"Can I use that trap gun up on the wall?"

"Nope. That gun too big for you. Now, when you gonna be able to haul some dirt so we can git the backdrop ready for the target range?"

"Listen, I can do about anything now, Skeeter, but first I want to teach you something."

"Boy, ain't nothin' I need at my age."

"Want to bet?"

"What you got to bet, Boy?"

"If I can find something to teach you that you don't know, you've got to let me use that trap gun when you think I'm ready."

"Boy, that gun gonna knock you on yo' behind."

"See, you've as good as admitted that I can find something you don't know. Come on outside. We've got something to show you."

"Uh-umm, you some determined soul."

Skeeter watched as the boys unloaded a funny-looking blue machine from the back of Steve's van. Skeeter thought the thing resembled a motorcycle, but it was too small. "What's that?"

"A moped," Joey answered as he brought the machine to the foot of the steps.

"A mo-what?"

"A moped. I can't ride it with my cast right now. We thought you could use it to go down and get your mail on the road. It's gas-powered and easier to ride than a bicycle."

"Boy, you be some mo-ron if you think this ole man gonna git hisself on that mo-ped! I could git these bones all broke up."

"Only if you don't pay attention to what you're doing. What have you got to lose by trying?"

"My life the first thing come to mind, Boy. I never even rode a bicycle."

"You've got to move with the times, Skeeter. What's the matter? You too old to learn something? You turn on the switch and use the key. Then you work the kicker and give it gas on the right handle. Nothing to it. When you want to stop, just put your feet down. Steve, show this chicken how it's done."

"There you go with that chicken business, Boy. Thought I done teached you better."

"Joe Louis isn't riding this. You are."

Skeeter shook his head as Steve started the moped. Steve drove slowly around the clearing, then increased his speed and circled the house. Watching the circling machine brought back long-suppressed feelings of deprivation. White children riding bicycles past big fancy houses came to mind as he remembered a youth spent with nothing more than a broken penknife. "Son, you really think this here man can ride that thing?"

"Yes, but you've got to be careful. It can turn over. Why don't you get on and let me push you around until you get the feel of it?"

"That the easiest way?"

"No, it's easier with the gas turned on."

"Son, if it easier turned on, then turn this mopedal on!"

"Are you sure you want to do this?"

"Git outta the way, Son, and let me ride!"

"Just remember to put your foot down to help you stop if you get in trouble," Steve added with concern.

"Son, git yo'self off and clear back!"

Skeeter sat on the machine waiting for the boys to get the moped started, then slowly he gave it gas. He wove around the yard, keeping every muscle at attention until he felt secure enough to increase his speed. Round and round he went until he thought he could venture around the house.

He passed the boys, circled once, then headed around again, ending the pattern in a figure eight. His back straightened. He held his head high. He was no longer an old man traveling like a boy. He was a boy, passing on the streets of town where he never dared venture. He was proud Robert Hawkins passing blue-eyed Mary Sue James as she stopped skipping rope on the sidewalk to watch in astonishment as the colored boy rode past in style. He waved to Howard Henry Dearing, the redheaded druggist's son who used to taunt him, as the boy stopped in midstreet to gaze longingly at Robert Hawkins on his moped. He passed all the white children in town, proud and regal, a poor young black boy riding like a king down their highway. Round and round he went, besting them all. He was heading down the country road of his memory to see his girl when he heard someone yelling, "Turn, Skeeter, turn!"

The voice sounded like his friend, Jubie Lotts. Skeeter knew that Jubie just wanted a ride on his fine machine, so he paid him no mind. Suddenly a blur raced in front of Skeeter's eyes, snapping his mind back to the present. The blur was not Jubie Lotts but Steve Foster racing to open a corral gate! Skeeter scooted through the gate with Steve screaming and pointing frantically at a mule who stood directly in the path! Skeeter skidded to a stop. While the mule brayed loudly in consternation, the old man wiped his forehead with a large white handkerchief. The boys ran over. Skeeter let out a breath and looked triumphantly around him.

"I done had me a fine ride on this mopedal! Yep, that postman gonna git the surprise of his life seein' me ridin' down that road in style. Guess you gonna be pesterin' me next 'bout that trap gun. Well, if I can keep from landin' on my backside, guess you can keep yo'self from bein' kicked on yo' behind, Boy. Still, you has to be ready."

"All right, Skeeter. Say, you did a heck of a job on that moped. We're real proud of you, aren't we, Steve?"

Steve held out his hand and shook Skeeter's while the mule continued to bray behind them.

"Now what's wrong with you, Franklin D. Roosevelt? Got to move with the times."

Franklin D. Roosevelt, not impressed, kept complaining loudly.

"Wonder what that ole mule's sayin' to me?"

"Skeeter," Joey said, "that old mule is telling you how you almost made a jackass out of yourself."

Eight

"Haul more dirt! This backdrop's ten feet high already!"

"Boy, shut yo' mouth and git to work!"

"Skeeter, I feel silly making birdcalls. Why do I need to sound like a mockingbird?"

"Son, when you huntin', you need to tell other hunters where you is without scarin' the animals. Maybe you like yellin' 'Hey, hunters! Here I is, and I see a deer!' "

"Skeeter, what do you think of this?"

"Boy, where the turtle? That thing look like a lizard."

"That's what it is. I started on the turtle, but somehow the shell just got thinner and thinner. Guess there was a lizard in that wood."

"Boy, you done killed the turtle, and that a sorry-lookin' lizard. Try agin."

"Skeeter, Franklin D. Roosevelt's gate latch is broken. I'm

going into town for a new one. Then we'll fix it."

"All right, Son. While you're at it, measure that chicken pen. Ole Joe Louis told me that wire gittin' awful rusty. Here some money to git the latch and the chicken wire."

"Skeeter, let's go for a walk."

"The last time we done went for a walk, Boy, you ain't had no mind to learn nothin'.

"Who needs to learn about silly flowers and trees?"

"You for one! Spring goin' by and them flowers and leaves'll be gone 'fore you git it into yo' head that you need 'em to find yo' way outta the woods. Course you done showed us how smart you is by steppin' down on a rotten limb and fallin' in a creekbed. If I's you, Boy, I'd look at lots of trees, so I could tell when they alive and when they dead!"

"We cut down the weeds around the pond. Now we're going to the shed. I've got that stock in a vise, and I want to finish it before it gets hot out there."

"All right, Son. Bring it in here if you git a problem."

"Skeeter, how does this look? I worked on it in study hall today."

"Workin' on this rabbit when you s'posed to be studyin'?"

"I had my work done. Besides, Skeeter, I'm carving a deer, not a rabbit."

"Then how come it got long, floppy ears?"

"Skeeter!"

"What's yo' goal with carvin', Boy?"

"Not to cut off my hand before you say I can stop."

110

"Set yo'self a goal. Pick out the animal you most like to do real good."

"I guess a dog."

"Then work good 'til you can do a dog. Then when you do that dog good, you be proud of yo'self."

"Should I start now?"

"No. Don't try a dog 'til you can do a deer."

"Man, it's hot. This .22's dripping."

"School almost out. Time for us to clear us off a beach by the pond. Got to git us some fishin' time. Let's see that rifle. Yep, it too wet. Go take that .270 off the wall."

"Say, how come Steve gets to use one of your guns? I'm ready for that trap gun like you promised!"

"Who say so, Boy? Git that twelve-gauge back together you has lyin' in the shed. Then show me it work. Then we see if you ready. One thing at a time, Boy."

The screen door slammed. "Skeeter, it's finished. Look," Joey said handing over the shotgun. "Who's ahead?"

"The Cardinals," Steve answered.

"Skeeter, I still don't understand why you won't let me bring that little TV out here, so we could watch the games instead of just listening to them."

"Boy, you can't look and work at the same time. That radio of yo's bad enough. Takes yo' mind out to some baseball diamond."

"You enjoy it, too. Course, you're a little behind the times. The Dodgers aren't in Brooklyn anymore."

"Don't be gittin' smart now, Boy," Skeeter replied as he

inspected the trigger. "I know the important stuff."

"Who do you think is the greatest baseball player ever?"

"Jackie Robinson. Thought you knowed that, Boy."

"I know he broke the color barrier, but that doesn't mean he's the greatest baseball player."

Skeeter looked at Joey in disgust. "Boy, you ain't understandin' the basics. You think baseball easy 'cause nobody paddin' up and bangin' into folks or jumpin' up under baskets like hounds after a treed possum. Can hide a body in them crowds. Baseball, now that just one man and his talent up in front of the world. Hard to show yo' stuff when folks throwin' bottles at you, callin' you names."

"You sure you aren't prejudiced?" Joey teased. "What about the great white players? Mickey Mantle, Pete Rose?"

"Them great, but like you say, them white."

"What about other black players? Hank Aaron, Frank Robinson?"

"Humph! You say this gun ready, and you can hit somethin' with it?"

"Just let me at it! I'm ready for that trap gun!"

"Son, you come work the trap for this great white hunter."

The three went outside and Joey positioned himself for his first shot. He missed when a bottle sailed into him.

"Skeeter, how come you threw that bottle at me?"

"Don't matter. A good shot ain't gonna be bothered by nothin' as silly as a little pop bottle."

Another clay bird sailed through the air, and Joey got a clean hit. His next shot was interrupted by a bottle striking him on the leg.

"Ouch! Come on, Skeeter!"

112

He turned around and repositioned his shotgun.

"You skinny, no-count, redneck, white trash! Git yo' cracker self off that firing line!" Steve released the bird, but Joey had lowered his gun.

"Why are you yelling at me, Skeeter? I can't concentrate. Besides, I'm not white trash or no-count or a cracker!"

"Jackie Robinson wasn't no nigger either, and they called him that. He hit the ball anyway."

"All right!" Joey yelled. "Jackie Robinson was the greatest baseball player who ever lived! Now will you watch me hit?"

"No. Go back to the shed and finish sanding down the stock of that shotgun. Then come back."

Joey stalked off in frustration while Skeeter and Steve returned to the cabin. They were busy eating cookies when Joey returned.

"Is this right now?" Joey asked as he handed the shotgun back to Skeeter.

"That sho' didn't take much time, Boy."

"It didn't need much time. I worked on it all morning. Hope you two saved some for me."

Steve handed Joey a cookie.

"Who did you say this target rifle belonged to?" Joey asked.

"The Judge's brother, Mr. Manly Broom Dodge."

"The same one who owned the trap gun from England I'm going to get to shoot?"

"Yep."

"Where did he get this gun?" Joey asked.

"Germany."

"He must have gone everywhere."

"Yep, he hop them oceans like they's puddles. Go ahead since you finally did this right, take down that trap gun. Mr. Manly Broom Dodge woulda liked you, Boy, 'cause you the same, full of sass and smiles. But Mr. Manly Broom did one thing at a time, be it women, travelin', shootin'."

"Did he have lots of women?"

"More than lots. One in every town, every continent."

"Then he didn't do women one at a time, did he?"

"Boy, when he with one woman, he concentrate so hard on her, she think she the onliest one in his life. Kept 'em off guard that way."

"And he was good with a shotgun?"

"The best. Now he could shoot anything, but the shotgun fit his personality. He had a bit of a twitch. He put it to use."

"I bet you didn't make him carve blocks of wood."

"Didn't make Mr. Manly Broom do nothin', but he coulda carved if he wanted. He tied his own trout flies. That take a lot of concentratin', Boy. Said it helped keep him calm. Times he wanted to be calm. Times he didn't. Them times was somethin' else. He could party like nobody I ever seen 'fore or since."

"How come you have his guns?" Joey asked as he took down the trap gun.

"He die young. I took care of him in his last days, and he give 'em back to me. I done the carvin' on both. Right proud of 'em. You can't fire that ole gun yet. Needs some work, but you can start on it."

Skeeter noticed the first glimmer of concentration in Joey's eyes. Intrigued by the story of the ladies' man, Joey cradled the gun with a fixed purpose in his mind. He was going to

114

shoot like Mr. Manly Broom Dodge. Skeeter had said that he was like him, and Joey had always pictured himself as something other than a gangly farm boy.

During the weeks that followed, Skeeter watched with interest as Joey showed that he was finally beginning to understand his own strengths. No longer did he complain about Steve's quiet abilities. Instead, Joey began to take pride in his own skill, and concentrated on the shotgun. Occasionally he jumped from task to task. Sometimes he still asked too many questions, and laughter was never far below the surface of his concentration, but Joey was clearly beginning to settle down. Whenever he became frustrated by poor shooting, he went inside the cabin and carved. When he was calm, he worked on the gun that belonged to Mr. Manly Broom Dodge. Thoughts of the shotgun's original owner became his passage to another world; tales of wealth and distant places carried him away from his humdrum life.

Skeeter told the boys a great deal about Mr. Manly Broom and his years with the Dodge family. The three fished frequently in Skeeter's pond, and the boys shared many of their own stories. The special time with him became the closest thing the boys knew to freedom that summer for their jobs kept them busy. Joey worked for his dad while Steve cleaned up around a construction site. Neither liked his work, and the long, hot hours were a period of endurance until the reward of lying in the shade beside Skeeter's fishing hole. Other friends badgered them to tag along, but the boys were protective of their relationship with Skeeter and respected the man's privacy.

Occasionally the Ryders sent food with Joey, and Charles

Ryder, worried that the boys were pestering Skeeter, dropped by to check. Skeeter had not met Steve's parents, but he was unconcerned. Then one day a car drove into the clearing, and a man got out. He bore a marked resemblance to Steve, and Skeeter knew that Duane Foster was paying him a visit.

"You must be Skeeter Hawkins," the man said when Skeeter came out on the porch.

"Yep," he replied.

"I'm Duane Foster, Steve's dad. My wife baked this for you," he said, holding out a chocolate cake. "She was going to send it with Steve, but I said I'd bring it."

"No call for yo' missus doin' that for me, but tell her I thank her," Skeeter said, taking the cake.

Silence hung heavy in the air until Duane Foster spoke. "I want you to know that we appreciate what you've done for Steve. He's a far better shot than I'll ever be, and he's gone from hardly knowing east from west to being a good tracker. What you've taught him has given him self-confidence, brought him out of himself. That's more important. I guess I've never been able to do that." He paused, searching for words.

"He's a fine boy. Natural rifleman."

"I'll have to admit that I didn't like the idea of him being out here at first. That's the way I was raised." Duane Foster looked up at Skeeter, but the placid look on Skeeter's face did not change.

"We don't worry about him now when he's with you. We know he couldn't be at a better place."

Skeeter knew the effort it had cost Duane Foster to confess his feelings, so he did not linger on the conversation. "Chocolate cake's my favorite. Thanks agin. I'll wait 'til them boys git here to eat it." He turned to go back inside the cabin.

"One more thing. Steve and Joey say that you're really particular. They don't think you'll buy this idea, but here it is. We've got a boat I picked up and repaired myself. I like doing that sort of thing. We don't need two boats, and I was wondering if you could use it."

"Give up on boats myself. Don't like to fall in the water, case I can't git out. But them boys might like it." Skeeter rubbed his chin. "Come to think of it, puttin' that blabby-mouthed boy in that boat and sendin' him out might git my ears some rest."

Duane Foster laughed. "You're right about Joey. He's a good kid, but he can get on your nerves. Still, you got him calmed down. Say, could I ask a favor?"

"Depends on the favor."

"Could I see Abraham Lincoln? Steve and Joey tell me he's some dog. But then I understand he's got a special trainer."

Skeeter thought for a second. "Abraham Lincoln!" he called inside the house. The dog appeared at the screen. "Got somebody here wants to see you. Them boys braggin' on you agin. Guess you'll want to show off with some of yo' tricks."

Nine

The hot August sun beat down mercilessly on the three fishermen stretched out on the bank of the pond. Each wore a Panama straw, but Joey's hat couldn't hide a mounting impatience. Finally, he gave up, laid aside his pole, and asked, "Skeeter, what do you know about women?"

"Boy, you best be askin' yo' daddy that stuff."

"I don't mean sex. I know all about that."

"Huh!" Steve said. "Skeeter, if you're smart, you'll make him get in the boat and row out to the middle of the pond before he gets started."

"Be quiet, Foster! I need to know this. Skeeter, I'm serious. We were roller skating last night, and there was this new girl at the skating rink. Man, was she a fox."

"I thought you seed yo'self a girl."

"Skeeter! She's a redhead with big blue eyes, and her figure would stop a clock. Do you think I should ask her out?"

"Depends."

"Depends on what?"

"Has she taken a shine to you? Don't go throwin' yo' pearls before no swine, no fox neither."

"I don't know. How can I tell if she's interested in me?"

"Has she got big cow eyes when you near?"

"Skeeter, that's not the part of her that looks like a cow," Steve said.

"Foster, shut up! What are cow eyes?"

"Big soulful eyes, starin' like you the onliest boy in her life."

"She hasn't met me but once. How do I get her cow-eyed?"

"Play hard to git. Make it where women beat a path to yo' door."

"I'd rather have them beat a path to the back seat of my car."

"Boy, has to git 'em in the car first. Then if you smart, them women'll drag you all over the upholstery."

"How do you play hard to get?"

"Do like I did with Suella Henderson. Started speakin' nicely to her at church picnics. Soon as she git comfortable, I flit off to speak to some other lucky girl. Yep, just buzzed from one to another like a bee. Suella got tired me speakin', never askin'. Finally she invite me over for chicken dinner. Had me some fine dinners in them days."

"Did you get Suella in the back seat?"

"Boy, that for me to know and Suella to remember. Now, this women business serious stuff. Lots of things ain't worth puttin' up with in the front seat just so you can hop in the back."

"Right now I'd put up with anything for some action."

"You just young and anxious. But take my word, Boy. Use yo' head. Learn how to spot them short runners."

"What?"

"Short runners. Women you only git hooked up with for a spell. Then you has to git unhooked 'cause you been dumb."

"How can you spot a short runner?"

"Can't always. Just you remember, no bossy women. Ain't no night in Heaven worth yo' day in Hell. Learned that fast with Suella. Uh-umm, she like to boss. Had enough folks tellin' me what to do without addin' her. 'Nother rule is run yo' eyes past the mama. Once had me this woman. God took a long time puttin' her together. Then I seed her mama. Hair all tied up, dress lappin' shut with a pin. That was it! That gal was out to catch me, then she go to the slops." Skeeter paused, so Joey asked, "That can't be all?"

"Nope. Just sortin' out my womenfolk. Can't talk 'bout 'em all." Skeeter rearranged his hat and continued. "Watch out for them gals with sweetness drippin' from their lips. They sneaky. Had me this one woman with honey lips. 'Yes, Skeeter.' 'No, Skeeter.' Then one time I come home and my house all covered with flowers and stuff moved 'round. That end that!"

"Maybe your place stunk, Skeeter."

"Shoot! Didn't even ask my permission! Just waltzed in and took over. No siree, I seen that gal gonna agree with me 'til I's hooked. Then she'd start changin' my life with a smile on her face. She got herself a real short run with Skeeter!"

"A short run's all I need with this redhead. How do I play hard to get? It'll be difficult for me because right now I'd be real easy."

"You say she new in town?"

"Yes."

"Then she don't know folks. School startin' next week.

You gonna make her think you the number-one catch!"

"Skeeter," Steve said. "That'd be a miracle."

"Son, you listen up now. You might learn yo'self something. Now, when that redhead come through that front door, Boy, you gonna be waitin' like you the doorman. Be polite, show her all 'round, but speak to all the girls. She start to think you the one to know. Now, don't stick like glue. Just when you git her feelin' good, take off after some other gal. Spread yo'self over the school like tar, git 'em all to stick. Pretty soon that redhead gonna think she better grab you for herself."

"What if she doesn't?"

"You ain't lost nothin'. Spreadin' yo'self 'round git all the women noticin' you. Might find somethin' better'n that rabbit."

"Fox, Skeeter, fox."

"Just do like I say, Boy. You gonna has yo'self a good time."

"If I'm lucky, she'll ask me to the Sadie Hawkins dance."

"Ain't no luck to it, Boy, if you listen to what I done said. Son, you mighty quiet. You has yo'self a fox?"

"Not worth the time, trouble, or money, Skeeter."

"Steve doesn't do a thing, Skeeter, and the women fall all over him! Last night he didn't ask one girl for a skate. They all asked him, and he didn't even care!"

"That's why. He don't care, and the women know it. He's bein' hard to git, just natural for him, Boy. Remember, no one pay no mind to that little perch waitin' to jump on yo' line. Them fish git caught and throwed back in 'cause everybody waitin' to snag that big fish. Just like me. Everybody want to land Skeeter Hawkins!"

"You sure don't lack ego, Skeeter."

"Just tellin' the truth, Boy."

"If you were so hard to catch, how come you got caught?"

"Found me a long runner."

"How could you tell?"

"Look at lots, Boy, you can tell the best. But first off, a woman got to be smart."

"I could use some help with my schoolwork."

"More to it than that, Boy. Now, my Loretta smart. She know how to play hard to git, too! Used to make me more'n one date on a Saturday night. Showed up at Loretta's place smellin' of another woman's party. Loretta take a hard look, one sniff, and screeches, 'Skeeter Hawkins! I'll thank you not to come over here reekin' of perfume and whiskey from another woman! You ain't no movie, and I ain't standin' in line!' Then she slam the door in my face."

"What did you do?"

"Asked her out agin. Knowed I had somethin' then. She say no. Asked her agin. She say no agin, then she change her mind. Ask me over to eat. I say no. Finally we started yessin' 'fore it too late."

"I don't know about a smart girl."

"You better learn. Smart women don't go rattlin' just to talk. Loretta always too busy 'bout her own business to flap her lips just bossin'. When she say somethin', it worth hearin'. That's the difference 'tween a smart and a bossy woman."

"Sounds like you really loved Loretta," Joey said.

"Yep. We had ourselves one good, long run. See, I found somebody I could respect. Neither of us never give the other reason to bow our heads in shame. Everybody respect Loretta. She always helpin' folks, seein' the good. Even when times was real bad, she would look up and find somethin' good. Don't git me wrong. Loretta never one of them silly folks thankin' the Lord for a foot bein' on their necks. Still, she knowed how to hold on to life. How to hold on to herself."

Skeeter said nothing for a time, and Steve peered up from under his hat to see if the old man was upset. He thought that Joey often overstepped himself, prying into people's lives, and he worried that Joey had hurt Skeeter by bringing up Loretta. When Skeeter did not appear upset, Steve relaxed and lay back down on the bank.

Joey continued, "Skeeter, what's the main thing I need to work on in order to attract girls?"

"Yo' twitch, Boy. Can't play hard to git if you bouncin' all over the place. Watch Son. Be cool, calm."

"That's gonna be hard for me. Maybe I should change my name. What do you think of Joe Ryder? That sounds more masculine and mature than Joey. Joey sounds like a baby. Maybe that's why I twitch. Maybe I wouldn't twitch if I was Joe."

"That's stupid," Steve said.

"No it's not! How many adult men do you know called Joey?"

"Then change your name when you're an adult," Steve answered. "If you go around now telling people that you're Joe Ryder, they'll just laugh. You're Joey to everyone and always have been."

"Well, I'm still going to think about it."

"You do that, Boy. You git serious 'bout all this women-folks business. Now this ole man gittin' serious about some sleepin'. Thinkin' 'bout all my women done plumb tuckered me out."

"If just thinking about them tires you out, you must have been exhausted when you were a ladies' man," Joey said.

"Some things don't never tire you out, Boy."

The boys laughed, then grew quiet. Steve went to sleep while Joey continued to stare up into the branches of the weeping willow. He was not certain he could play hard to get, and he was not even positive he wanted to try. After all, he had gone to the same schools with the same people for years without changing anything. If he took Skeeter's advice and curbed his playful enthusiasm, his classmates might think he was acting dumb. Being Joey Ryder was hard enough without being considered a stupid Joey Ryder, and he thought Steve was probably right. He was not yet Joe. Still, try as he might, Joey could think of no other plan for attracting the new girl, and for some mysterious reason, she excited him. Since Skeeter was usually right, Joey decided to try playing hard to get.

A week later Joey faithfully followed Skeeter's instructions. He calmly greeted the new girl at the front door and showed her the school, pointedly speaking to every female he saw. If the object of his attention was not captivated by Joey, she opened up the world of flirtation to him, and he knew he was on to something big.

"Skeeter, I did it," Joey said. "Week one, the redhead. I've got her interested. This week, week two, it's Bobbie Anne Lebel. We're meeting at the football game. I never thought she'd turn out so good after elementary school."

"Well, imagine you wasn't such a hot dog then either, Boy. How about you, Son?"

"Nothing yet, Skeeter, but I'm looking. Can we do something for you?"

"Yep, finish nailin' down them shingles on the shed. I started, couldn't finish. Got too winded."

"Come with us, and I'll tell you all about Bobbie Anne!"

However, the next week Joey reported, "Skeeter, forget Bobbie Anne. Week three, and it's time to move on."

"You want to move on to some targets?"

"Sure. Will you work the trap?"

"No, let Son do it. I'll just sit and watch. Any more women to report?"

"I'll tell you when there is."

Several days later, the boys came rushing into the house. Skeeter was sleeping in his chair, but he quickly woke up when Joey announced, "Week four, and we've won the sweepstakes! I asked out the redhead, and Steve has a date with Betty Smith, a real fox. What do you think?"

"Don't surprise me none," Skeeter said softly. "You boys gittin' growed. Both shot up, gittin' meat on yo' bones, smellin' of stink most of the time. Tell me about them gals."

The boys began to talk. Skeeter listened quietly. He enjoyed hearing tales of their exploits, never begrudging the time they spent with their friends, even when it took time away from him. When they did visit, he often needed their help.

"Skeeter, I've got the truck outside," Joey said one day. "Even though it's week seven and countdown to the Sadie Hawkins dance, let's go fix that fence."

Joey hurried back to the truck, assuming Skeeter would be right behind him. But the boys watched as Skeeter slowly descended the steps and crept toward them.

"Skeeter, are you all right?" Joey asked. "You sure are dragging today."

"Yep, I am, Boy. But let's git to that fence."

The boys worked while Skeeter watched from the truck. They took him home, intending to check on him. But week eight was a banner time with a football game and several parties, so they didn't check. On their next visit, Skeeter seemed all right except for being cranky.

Then one day late in October they arrived to find Skeeter so tired that he could not even concentrate on what Joey was telling him.

"Skeeter, look at this," Joey said as he held out a small carving. "I know you think I've given up carving for women, but look at this. If this isn't a deer, I don't know what it is. Of course, it's not finished."

Skeeter nodded.

"You know, carving comes in handy with women. I've passed out several wooden hearts. Guess what! Countdown time is over for Steve. He got asked to the Sadie Hawkins dance by one of the foxes of the junior class."

Skeeter rubbed his forehead lightly and quietly said, "You goin', Son?"

"You bet, Skeeter. Ask Joey about his date."

"You got one?" Skeeter forced himself to say, his eyes almost covered by heavy lids.

"A girl asked, but I don't want to go with her. Besides, I have to work. Skeeter, you're now looking at an employed man. I got that job at the Fair Deal Grocery, the one I told you about. I have to work all day Saturdays, two days after school, and one night a weekend. The manager thinks Steve can get on soon. You should see the check-out girls!"

Skeeter's head dropped. The boys exchanged worried glances. "Skeeter, are you all right?" Steve asked.

"Just tired. These bones achin' today."

"We can take you to a doctor."

Skeeter waved away the suggestion.

"Skeeter!" Joey said. "You just can't sit here if you're sick!"

"Then you boys help me lie down."

The two helped Skeeter to the side of his iron bed where he sat down, pulled out his white handkerchief, and wiped his face.

"Skeeter," Joey asked to draw the man's attention away from their concern. "What's wrong with Franklin D. Roosevelt? He was braying like all get-out when we drove out. Now he's at it again."

"That ole mule givin' out like me. You git that vet to tend him. Now I need to lie down."

The boys helped Skeeter position himself. Joey looked thoughtful for a moment, then said, "You're more concerned about that old mule than you are about yourself."

"Boy, I be responsible for that mule."

"Well, I'm taking responsibility for the old mule on this bed. I'm going to get my mother!"

Joey walked out of the cabin before anyone could respond. Skeeter closed his eyes while Steve nervously paced the floor. He hated being around sick people because he never knew what to do. He looked around the cabin for something to pass the time while thoughts of the possibility of Skeeter's dying hammered away in his mind. He took the .22 down from the wall and sighted the gun on the far window.

Skeeter softly called, "Jerry, yo' chores done?"

Startled by the man's confusion, Steve hoped that the sound of his voice would bring Skeeter back to the present. "Yes, Skeeter. I'm just looking at Jerry's .22."

"Know you don't think much of that gun," the voice whispered. "But that gun gonna look good when the army finish with you."

"Skeeter, you know I love this gun."

"Piddlin' work. That's what you call my carvin'. But carvin' help me stand tall, even if I's standin' in the white man's shadow."

"Skeeter! Skeeter!" Steve said. "It's me, Steve! Steve Foster! Remember me?"

The figure stirred slightly, and the voice slowly resumed. "I live my times my way. You live yo' times yo' way. Won't be no times if you git killed."

Steve moved to the end of the bed, hoping he could get Skeeter to open his eyes and recognize him. Frightened, he asked, "Skeeter, Skeeter, are you all right? Skeeter, it's me, Steve! Skeeter, please answer me!"

Now the old man neither answered nor moved. Steve gripped the cold bed railing until his palms throbbed. He saw no signs of life, and thought that he had let Skeeter slip away without saying good-bye. Steve pleaded, "Skeeter, Skeeter, please speak to me!" Skeeter's chest rose in response, and Steve moved to his side, reached out, and grasped Skeeter's arm. Skeeter's eyes slowly opened. Surprise, then slow recognition, came into the wrinkled face.

"Son, that you? Musta been dreamin'."

"Am I glad you're awake. How do you feel?"

"Tired, Son, tired. Why the mopey face?"

"You gave me a real scare, Skeeter."

"Don't fret none, Son. These bones ain't gonna gather in the mornin'." Steve looked confused. "Times I forgit, Son. You bein' white mean you don't always git this ole man. Don't fret none," the old man whispered. "I ain't gonna die yet." Skeeter closed his eyes.

Relieved, Steve listened to the old man's labored breathing. He thought back to the first visits with Skeeter and remembered with shame the embarrassment he had felt in the black man's presence. The two of them had come a long way together, and Steve realized that their journey would end, never to repeat itself. No one, not even his father, understood him as well as Skeeter Hawkins. The unquestioning acceptance the old man extended to him was a luxury no one else in his life would be able to afford. Suddenly, without embarrassment or shame, Steve sat on the edge of the iron bed and held the gnarled hand until the Ryders' lights shone in the clearing.

Faye Ryder had no more luck than the boys in convincing Skeeter to see a doctor. However, Skeeter allowed her to organize the next twelve hours while he obediently sat up in bed and ate her food.

"Mr. Hawkins, I wish you'd let us get a doctor, but since you won't, I'll call Mrs. Jackson. Joey thinks you can train Abraham Lincoln to come for us in an emergency. Will you do that? From what I hear, I'd probably be better off taking that dog home and leaving Joey with you. I can't train him to do anything."

Skeeter smiled.

"I'll wrap up the rest of this casserole, so you can eat it later."

"Thank you, ma'am."

"Skeeter, I'll stay here until Mrs. Jackson comes," Joey offered.

"You boys lock up the guns in the hidin' place. Don't want to worry about them when I'm down. Do that, then go. The dogs and me be fine."

When the boys had finished, Joey said, "We're going, Skeeter. I'll stop by tomorrow on my way to school."

Skeeter nodded drowsily.

On their way to the car, Joey questioned his mother. "I don't know what's wrong with him," she answered. "A mild stroke perhaps, or his heart. My grandpa used to have spells when he just gave out. I do know one thing. For his age that old man is remarkable, and you boys expect far too much from him."

On the way to the Ryders, the boys decided to check on Skeeter frequently and hoped the tired spell would pass.

Joey drove up the next morning, and he was pleased to see Skeeter fixing the dogs' breakfast.

"Ain't they havin' school today, Boy?"

"I'm on my way, Skeeter. How are you feeling? You look better."

"Feel fine today. Thank yo' mama agin."

"Did your sister-in-law get over?"

"Yep. She just left. Fanny's good at doctorin' my miseries."

130

"You have those spells often?"

"Every now and then. Lately been more now than then."

"Are you sure you shouldn't see a doctor?"

"Boy, these ole bones just tired carryin' me 'round on this earth. Ain't nothin' no doctor can do 'bout that."

"You'll let us train Abraham Lincoln, won't you? I've even got a command. You liked Mom's casserole, so let's get him to our place with 'Tater Tots Casserole'."

"Heared worse. Y'all do the work. I can train the dog."

"Sure, Skeeter. Say, which vet do you want me to get out here? Doc Haskell or that new man?"

"Don't need no vet now. Franklin D. Roosevelt lots better today. He just got a touch of the miseries, too. Doc Haskell done told me to git rid of that mule. Just like swattin' a fly to him to send that ole mule off this earth. No siree, that ole mule a part of me."

"All right. Steve and I decided to skip the women talk. We figure we brought on your spell by causing you to remember your past," Joey kidded. "You just got worn out thinking about Suella and the rest."

"Probably so, Boy."

"I'll stop by after school."

"Boy, you gonna tire my eyes out. Still, I 'preciate yo' blabby self. Takin' spells when you ain't so blabby. You don't even ask question, question, question. Must have learned somethin'. Yes sir, times you gittin' to be Mister Joe."

"Mister Joe? That sounds like a hamburger joint. I think I'll stick to Joey."

"Thanks agin for last night."

"You're welcome, Skeeter. See you this afternoon."

Ten

"Tater Tots Casserole!"

Abraham Lincoln bounded off in the direction of the Ryders', and Steve nodded his head in approval as the dog disappeared. Skeeter rocked on the porch as if nothing had happened, but fifteen minutes later Abraham Lincoln reappeared riding triumphantly in the truck beside Joey.

"Skeeter, what do you think?" Joey called, climbing down from the pickup. "Abraham Lincoln probably set a record running to our place."

"Humph!"

"I see we've got the cranks again. Come on, Skeeter."

"Come on nothin', Boy! Git that dog outta that truck 'fore he git the notion all he got to do in life is catch hisself a ride."

"I tried to get him back with 'collard greens,' " Joey said, "but he said he was sick of soul food!"

Ignoring Joey's remark, Skeeter slowly pushed himself out of the rocker. "Son, git Jackie Robinson back over here. Time to teach him to carry that bird right!"

Steve put his fingers to his mouth and whistled loudly.

The Labrador raced out from the broad green leaves and ran eagerly toward the boys, barking out his greetings. While they waited for Jackie Robinson, Joey thumbed in question at the porch, and Steve answered with a nod of his head: Skeeter was having another bad day.

The old man had not suffered again from the miseries, but he was becoming increasingly marked by age. He had his good days, laughing, joking, and running the small property. On the bad days, he moved with a pained shuffle and he sullenly withdrew, snapping irritably at the boys. Skeeter's miseries often coincided with bad weather. That morning Skeeter had searched the overcast sky, and Steve asked him what was wrong.

"Winter comin'."

"That means we can hunt."

"Y'all can hunt. Cold cause these bones of mine to pain."

"Can't you take some medicine?"

"Can't take no medicine for bein' too old."

Usually if Joey persisted, he could joke Skeeter out of the doldrums, but today not even Joey was having any luck. The two boys stood by quietly with Jackie Robinson. Skeeter stared at the sky again, then started slowly down the steps. Steve hurried up to offer assistance. "Son, I done told you a thousand times. Ain't no need for you helpin' me do nothin'. Y'all thinkin' this ole man half dead!"

"Half dead?" Joey answered. "I swear I passed someone who looked just like you heading for the Oaks Cemetery with a big frown on his face. I thought you'd kicked off! I'm just here to steal Joe Louis for dinner."

Skeeter gave Joey a sharp look. Then his gaze softened,

"Boy, St. Peter hisself gonna stop you at them pearly gates 'cause of yo' sass." The old man continued his slow walk, but the boys relaxed when they noticed a wry smile on Skeeter's face. Soon he was acting more like himself.

"Sorry this ole man so poorly. Guess at times ole Skeeter right bad comp'ny."

"Skeeter, you're always good company. Sometimes you're a little cranky."

"Well, Boy, sometimes I's just a little crippled. My legs won't git me places fast like they used to. Some days they don't even work!"

"You're still remarkable for your age, Skeeter."

"Don't want to be remarkable, Boy. Movable, now that interest me. My legs goin'. My hands ain't workin' too good. I worry what gonna go next."

"Why don't you see a doctor?" Joey asked.

"What he gonna do for me, Boy? Give me new legs? Even with new legs, my insides wore out. Times my brain don't git me enough blood to think."

"Well, let's see how your brain is working now. Guess what's coming up next week?"

"Boy, I hardly know what comin' up tomorrow."

"Quail season opens, and it's our one-year anniversary. You'd better get ready because we're hot to hit those fields!"

"Don't see how y'all goin' to have time with workin', goin' to school, and flyin' in and out of here like mockin'birds after an ole cat. Keep my ears tired listenin' to tires burnin' up my drive. Done taught you boys proper huntin' take time."

"The two of us are coming over next Sunday at one o'clock and heading out right after the party. We're bringing the food, so all you need to do is blow up the balloons," Joey said.

"Boy, you the one with air for balloons. You got 'nough for a blimp!"

"Funny, Skeeter. Listen, the manager said he'll try to schedule Steve and me together, so we can have the same afternoons off. You might get tired having us back here together so much."

"Seem to me y'all here right much. Just don't light long enough to swat a fly, but suit yo'selves. I be here."

Skeeter's comments told the boys that he did not suspect the two were checking on him. Joey had been stopping by frequently on his way to school while Steve drove over at least two afternoons a week. Usually their visits were brief and made separately on different days. They seldom hunted. When they did, the boys brought along their own food, which they shared with Skeeter. If the old man was having a bad day, they remained only a short time.

When they arrived on the following Sunday for the anniversary celebration, Skeeter appeared to be having an average day. The boys had food packed in a white oak basket, and Joey removed a barrel of chicken and a box of Twinkies.

"Looks like you got food for two days."

"My mother griped me out when she saw me loading up this basket. She said it was a work of art and shouldn't be used. I told her that of course it was a work of art. I cut every split in this basket, and that's why I'm using it."

"You take care of that basket, Boy, and it'll be around long as you."

"Say, Skeeter," Steve said, "there's a yellow cat under the shed nursing three kittens."

"Don't know nothin' 'bout no cat."

"I saw her when I went to replace that oil I needed. She's curled up under the step with three kittens."

"Where's A. Philip Randolph?" Joey asked.

"That ole cat's off on one of his trips. Left this place unguarded. That mama cat done stole on my property. Ain't got no right bringin' this ole man trouble."

"Trouble?" Joey said. "What's one more cat in the country? Besides, A. Philip Randolph's probably gotten hitched without telling you."

"This pet shop closed up," he said sternly. "Don't want no more animals. The ones 'round here all old and tired like me."

"And grumpy," Joey added.

"Humph!"

"Come on, Skeeter, we can at least name your animals."

"Son, they ain't my animals!"

"What can naming them hurt?"

"Boy, givin' 'em a name mean they got yo' attention. Then you stuck."

"We'll take care of getting rid of them if you'll just let us show them to you."

Joey went after the small litter. He thought the sight of the tiny animals might perk Skeeter up.

"We'll each name a kitten," he announced and lowered the cardboard box in front of Skeeter.

"I know you want the black one. Steve, which one do you want?"

"I want the blonde."

"Blonde?" Skeeter said. "That yellow kitten ain't no

blonde! If that kitten be a blonde, then this here black one be a brunette, and it ain't nothin' but an ole black cat."

"Come on, Skeeter," Joey said. "That black kitten's frisky. Look at him push his way in."

Two of the kittens were nursing. Left out, the black kitten pushed and struggled until he too had found a place. Skeeter looked satisfied.

"What are you going to name him, Skeeter?"

"Boy, I best check to see that this be a he and not a she cat." Skeeter pulled the kitten away and held it up. He replaced his choice with a pleased expression.

"That there be Martin Luther King, Jr. Bound to git his fair share, pushin' if he has to."

"Sounds good, Skeeter. Steve, what's yours?"

"Tammy."

"Tammy! That ain't no name for a cat," Skeeter protested.

"No, but it's the name of a girl," Joey said.

"Oh."

"You'd better check to see if that yellow cat is a female," Joey said, "or else some tomcat's going to have an identity crisis. Impressed, Skeeter? I learned that in psychology class." Before Skeeter could respond, Joey slapped his back jeans pocket and continued, "Say, Skeeter, I almost forgot! You've got to help me with a psychology assignment!"

"What's that?"

"It's a class I'm taking at school about what makes people tick. Right now we're studying the psychology of aging, and I'm supposed to interview an older person. I figure I can't get much older than you and still have the person breathing."

"Thanks, Boy, but I dunno. This sickology stuff news to me."

"You don't have to know anything. Just answer the questions I have when we get back."

"Maybe I best answer them now while I's still breathin'."

"Nope. We want to get in those fields. But first check the sex of this kitten."

Skeeter took one look. "Female."

"That's Sex Kitten," Joey said.

"Boy, you some kind of sick namin' a poor cat that."

"Listen, Skeeter. If she lives up to her name, she'll be the hottest thing in the barn. See you later."

"Y'all be careful. Don't be blowin' off yo' toes just to has a target."

The boys spent the afternoon prowling the fields with Jackie Robinson and Abraham Lincoln. Neither spoke of Skeeter or of the year that had passed, but each felt that he was in transit from the boy he had been. But whatever became of them as men, some things they had first experienced as boys would never change; the friendship, the feel of the outdoors, the beauty of the sky, and the freedom of the surrounding fields would always be the same.

They hunted with some success until the sun began to set, then returned to the cabin. Skeeter critically examined their birds as he always did, but they still enjoyed his comments. While Steve unpacked the chicken, Joey pulled a rumpled paper from his back pocket and smoothed out the wrinkles.

"Skeeter, let's do these questions now. Here, have a Twinkie." Joey sat down, and Jackie Robinson crawled into his lap.

"Boy, this some kind of assignment. A grubby piece of

paper and you sittin' there with yo' mouth full of food and yo' lap full of dog. I guess Jackie Robinson interested in sickology?"

"I've thought of sending him to class for me, but I probably couldn't read his notes. First question. How old are you?"

"Real old."

"Come on, Skeeter. What can telling your age hurt?"

"Joey!" Steve said.

"All right. I'll put you're over ninety. Now what is the first historical event you remember? I expect you knew George Washington personally."

"Close, but not quite. We lived so far back in the sticks I hardly knowed there was a world 'til I's 'bout eight. Guess I first recall folks talkin' 'bout President Roosevelt."

"Franklin?" Joey asked.

"No, Teddy."

"Third question."

"Did we finish the second?"

"I put down Roosevelt."

"Boy, he a person, not an event."

"Close enough. Now when did you cast your first vote, for whom, and why?"

"That a mouthful, Boy."

"It's also a stupid question," Steve said.

"Why?"

"You saw that movie at school last year. Blacks couldn't vote in the South until the sixties." Steve was concerned that Joey was again trespassing into Skeeter's private life. "Maybe he doesn't want to answer that stuff."

"Son, you mostly right. Most colored folks couldn't vote.

'Round here things' diff'rent. All the colored here just rounded up like cattle, trucked to the polls, voted like they's told. Ain't no choice, no way. Never voted then. Nobody gonna tell me how to vote. Once the Judge asked me why I ain't showed up to the polls, and I told him I ain't planned on goin' down. He never asked me agin."

"So you've never voted?"

"Voted the first time when I seen change comin'. 1964 I voted for Lyndon Baines Johnson. Was an old man then."

"Next question. Do you think you've accomplished your goals or do you still have goals you want to achieve?"

"Guess I 'complished my goal. I kept alive to answer these silly questions. In my day stayin' alive was a real goal."

"What do you think of the younger generation?"

"Which one? At my age all generations is younger."

"Oh, I guess our generation."

"You and Son all right. Don't speak for nobody I don't know and don't know many folks now. But can't expect things to stay like they was. Can't hold the young to old ways."

"What would you change about your life if you could live it over again?"

"Scratch that question, Boy."

"What can I put?"

"What color yo' teacher?"

"White."

"Figures."

"Why?"

"Humph! You tell yo' teacher I say nobody need to ask that question of an ole colored man from these parts. Anybody don't know why, tell 'em the answer is writ on the hangin' tree."

Joey wrote down the answer without comment. "The teacher said that if we had a good interview we might ask about dying."

"Joey, just skip that part."

"Skeeter doesn't care, Steve. Skeeter, my teacher said it might upset some old people to talk about death."

"Dyin' upset *young* folks, Boy. Ole people s'posed to die."

"I know, but aren't you afraid?"

"Nope."

"That's your answer?"

"Yep. Boy, I live with dyin' all my days. Good dyin', bad dyin', men dyin', animals dyin', dyin' for right, dyin' for wrong, dyin' for no good reason, dyin' for the wrong reason. Death and me be friends. Some day you understand if you live a good, strong life with not much to shame you. Now when y'all gonna offer me some of that chicken?"

Joey's interview with Skeeter marked the end of serious conversation for several weeks. The new schedule at the grocery store allowed the boys to hunt together regularly, and they showed up faithfully at the cabin. Generally, Skeeter seemed to have more good days than bad, but the boys thought that perhaps they were simply growing accustomed to his cranky spells. Then one Wednesday afternoon the two drove over after school and found Skeeter slumped down in his rocker with a scowl on his face. Joey cautiously approached Skeeter and pulled a small, carved dog out of his pocket.

"Skeeter, I finished my dog. What do you think?"

The old man hardly glanced at the dog.

"It's yours. I'll put it right here on this stand. When you feel better, I want your opinion. Who knows? I might have done so well you'll be badgering me about carving a whole kennel full of dogs. Actually, I'm starting to enjoy carving now that I'm no longer carving lizards."

Skeeter did not respond to Joey's humor, so the boy shook his head and stepped back in frustration.

"Skeeter, is Abraham Lincoln ready to go?" Steve asked.

"No!"

The boys exchanged glances, and Steve tentatively asked, "Why not, Skeeter?"

"He ain't goin' huntin' 'til you boys get rid of them kittens!"

"Now?" Joey asked. "We were going—"

"You heared me, Boy!"

"I'll go right now and get them!" Joey said.

"Skeeter, are you all right?" Steve asked when Joey left the room. Skeeter did not answer as he stared stonily into his lap. When Joey opened the door, Steve tried to signal him to keep quiet, but the boy was already talking.

"Skeeter, are you sure you don't want to keep Martin Luther King, Jr.? See how frisky he's gotten?" He lowered the box to where Skeeter could see, but the old man refused to look. Joey tried again, "You sure you don't want him?"

"Yep. Git rid of 'em," Skeeter answered firmly.

"Suit yourself, Skeeter. I'll take Sex Kitten and Martin Luther King, Jr. A girl in my class wants a kitten, and I'll just keep the other one in the barn until I find a home. Steve, are you still giving the yellow kitten to your girl?"

Steve nodded.

"And who might that be?" Skeeter asked with his first tone of interest.

"Tammy Northcutt."

"That Jack Northcutt's girl?"

Steve nodded, then grew uneasy for the face he saw was twisted in hate.

"Skeeter, I'm not certain of her father's name —"

"Her daddy a doctor?"

"Yes. So's her granddad. They own a clinic out —"

"I know all about 'em! Put that box back under the house! I'll drown them kittens myself!"

"Drown them!" Joey protested. "Skeeter, you don't need to kill them!"

Steve took hold of the cardboard box and tried to pull it from Joey's grasp. He had no intention of arguing with Skeeter and planned to get out of the house as quickly as possible, but Joey would not let go. He continued, "Skeeter, we'll get rid of the cats. If you don't want Tammy Northcutt to have one, we won't give her the yellow cat. I'll take all of them." Skeeter's face relaxed, then Joey made the mistake of adding, "It's nothing to get upset over."

The remark unleashed a torrent of emotion within Skeeter. He thrust his finger at Joey and shouted, "Nothin' to git upset over! It ain't nothin' to you! Ain't never been nothin' to you folks! But it somethin' to me! My family somethin' to me! My time somethin' to me! Y'all think I should be flattered you give this poor ole colored man some of yo' precious time, yo' precious white time! But that not how I got it figured, Boy!"

Steve grabbed Joey's upper arm in a vain attempt to quiet

143

him, but Joey was determined to right the wrong he felt was being done to him.

"Skeeter, that's not what we think, and you know it! Obviously, you've hated Northcutt's guts for some —"

"Hate Northcutt? Hate ain't strong enough. Boy! He let my Loretta die! Let her lay there and die while he tend his white patients!" Skeeter stopped for a breath, then continued. "Course, what one more dead colored woman! They don't count for nothin'! I teached Northcutt how to shoot when he a youngun. Used to hear him go 'round braggin' how good he could shoot 'cause I teached him. Used to hear Northcutt call me his friend. Then when I need my good friend, he happen to remember ole Skeeter colored. Too bad, 'cause Skeeter was one fine teacher, but we can't have them colored git outta their place! They might git ideas! Why, colored might git to thinkin' they as good as white folks! Can't have that now, can we, Boy?"

Skeeter spat the question at Joey, who answered, hurt but determined. "Skeeter, I'm sorry, but I didn't have anything to do with what happened then."

"Didn't have nothin' to do with it! Yo' kind never have nothin' to do with it!"

The old man and the boy stared angrily at each other. Steve tried once again to get Joey to move by pulling on the box, but Joey would not budge.

Skeeter was determined to pin blame on someone, and Steve knew that Joey never accepted the blame for anything, even when he was clearly at fault. Skeeter pushed himself forward out of his chair and looked straight into Joey's eyes. "You got something to say to me, Boy?"

"Skeeter, believe me, whatever happened back then I'd change if I could, but I can't."

Skeeter lowered himself back into his chair, muttering bitterly, "You right, Boy. You can't change nothin'!"

The boys hoped that Skeeter's temper would cool, but he looked up and started in again on Joey. "You ask about my life, Boy. You ask what I'd change, as if a colored man could change one tiny thing. Well, I'll tell you what I'd change! If I could just change one thing, I'd have my boy back! I'd have my Jerry, and he'd stand up tall and straight! You hear me, Boy?"

"Yes, Skeeter," Joey said. "That would be nice."

"Nice! That would be nice! You think havin' him back would be nice! No, Boy! I'd have my son back, and he'd stand tall and straight, and he'd yell, 'Come on, Bull Connor! Turn on them hoses! You got yo'self a man this time!'" Skeeter's call rent the air. His eyes were fixed on something only he could see. "And I'd watch that TV screen, and I'd be proud seein' my boy holdin' on to that tree, holdin' on like a man. Yes, Bull Connor! You got yo'self a man this time!"

The boys stood, rigid, as the sounds echoed in the room. Skeeter was no longer with them. They waited until he came back to the present. Joey quietly asked, "Skeeter, who's Bull Connor?"

Skeeter buried his face in his hands. The boys nodded their heads in agreement to leave. Then they heard muffled sounds that were unrecognizable, coming as they did from Skeeter Hawkins. The two looked down. First they were amazed, then embarrassed, and finally concerned as they listened to the long sobs that tore through the man. Steve gently pulled the box from Joey's hand and set it down on the floor. He leaned over and put his hand on Skeeter's back. Joey knelt beside the rocker and tried to touch Skeeter's knee, but the old man brushed him away.

"Skeeter," Steve said. "Is there something we can do?"

Skeeter shook his head and continued crying into his hands.

"Skeeter, please tell us what's wrong," Steve said.

The old man tried to talk, but he choked on his words. Finally, the boys made out what he was trying to say.

"Son," Skeeter sobbed. "I know I lived past my time. But I done lived past my boy's time, too." He did not look at the boys. "You boys just git out! Just git out!"

Steve lifted the box and motioned Joey to go ahead. "Skeeter," he said, "we're going. You send Abraham Lincoln to Joey when you want us back."

"Don't want ya'll back!"

"Send him if you change your mind."

The boys opened the door and left.

Eleven

A week later Abraham Lincoln barked at the Ryders' back door. Skeeter had attached a note to his collar asking the boys to return the following day. Joey was relieved Skeeter had written, for his anger had left the boys wondering how they could continue the friendship. Words of apology did not right past wrongs nor restore to Skeeter what he had lost, so they had simply waited.

"Y'all sit down. Time to talk," Skeeter said as he greeted them. The boys could tell that he was no longer angry.

"The other day was bad. Sorry for what I done. Didn't have no call to go yellin' 'bout things don't have nothin' to do with y'all. Don't do nobody no good."

"I think it did," Steve said. "We learned something."

"Yeah, we sure know who Bull Connor is now," Joey said. "We looked him up. He was Commissioner of Police in Birmingham in 1963 when they used fire hoses on the civil rights marchers."

"That he was. Still, yellin' ain't a good way to teach."

"You hadn't yelled at us until then, even the times when we probably needed it. Don't worry about what happened."

"Nice of you, Son. Times the miseries come over me. Been comin' right much lately. I don't mind the hurtin' so, but can't stand becomin' a mean ole man —"

"Aw, Skeeter."

"Boy, quiet yo'self. Said yo'selves I's cranky, even 'fore the other day. Then I was so cranky I wouldn't even look at yo' dog." Skeeter pointed at the small carving sitting next to his pipe. "It's a good dog, too. I's pleased with it, Boy. That dog gonna sit right there and guard my pipe. But I didn't git y'all over here just to talk 'bout dogs. I been thinkin' things over, and now I know it time."

"Time for what?"

"Time to go on the big hunt, Boy. Y'all almost growed. Come in here smellin' of stink with yo' shirttails tucked in. Both toppin' out over six feet. Even you, Boy, ain't twitchin' so much. Soon, you boys have no more need of this ole man." He looked calmly at Steve and Joey. "And this ole man won't be needin' you two." Skeeter let the boys reflect on his words as he loaded his pipe and lit the tobacco. "That day you shot the rabbit I's walkin' 'round feelin' sorry for myself. I heared the gun, got mad. Folks ain't s'posed to hunt my land. Then I seen you two. I's fixin' to really let y'all have it. Then somethin' struck me. You two reminded me of my other two boys. I stopped, thought. Still mad then, but not at y'all."

"You sure had us fooled if you weren't mad at us," Joey said.

"Didn't have nobody 'cept Fanny and Shirley. They no good huntin' and shootin', so I ask the good Lord to send me somebody. Forgot to ask for my own kind. Thought he'd know that! See, I give my whole life, my skill, my time, mostly to whites. Didn't like all them whites. Wanted my people to git what's left of this ole man. When you showed up, I was angry. Said, 'Lord, I know You colorblind, but this ridiculous. White boys!' So that's why I brung you home. Had to find out for myself if you the ones sent. Didn't take me long to know you was."

"How did you know?" Steve asked.

"Yo' interest. Could hardly take yo' eyes off them guns, Son. And Boy was so friendly and got so many questions, I knowed he'd come back to talk about 'em. Then it seemed good havin' you two here."

"Do you call me Son because I remind you of Jerry?"

"Not really. It just felt right. Lots of old folks call men they like son. You ain't Jerry. Boy ain't Peter Dodge. Each of you put his own footprint on this earth. But there is things similar in them two and y'all. Jerry was the rifleman. He was calm, quiet, keepin' it all inside like you, Son. When you hold yo' gun, the confident way you stand call Jerry to my mind. Peter was the shotgun man. He and Boy both full of sass and smiles. That first day Boy just jumped right in to explain hisself. That Peter's way. And stubborn. One time he went out huntin' in a storm 'cause he mad at me. He fell down, broke his ankle, and we had to send the dogs out after him. Just like we did this ornery thing."

"Glad somebody else was that stupid," Joey said.

"He not stupid, just stubborn and careless. That's why we worked on slowin' you down, makin' you be patient. Now you got it, and now it time to go to the Big Boggey."

149

"The Big Boggey! It's been drained!"

"Not where we're goin', Boy. Not where he waitin'."

"Who's he?"

"Him." Skeeter calmly pointed to the .30-30 on the wall. Steve felt a chill but said nothing.

"Him who, Skeeter? I don't see anyone."

"Tell him, Son."

"The buck," Steve answered nervously.

"A buck? You want to go deer hunting?"

"Yep. Time to go 'fore you two git growed and leave. Time to go while these ole bones can still carry me 'round."

"Why do we have to go all the way to what's left of the Big Boggey for a deer?"

"I just want to go back."

"Why?"

"Because that's where the buck is. That's where he waitin' for me."

Joey sat quietly for a moment looking suspiciously at Skeeter. Then he looked at the rifle, then back at Skeeter. "Skeeter! You can't mean that we're going after that buck on the rifle! He's got to be dead!"

"He puffin' like me, but he waitin' like me."

"How do you know?"

"Don't know for sure, Boy, but I bet he there. I feel it in my bones."

Joey shook his head. "None of this is making sense! First, you want to go hunting in a place that doesn't exist! Second, you want to hunt a deer who's ancient and probably not alive!"

"Boy, Skeeter old, but Skeeter here, ain't he?"

"If by some remote possibility he's as old as you, he's probably in the same shape, in which case it would be criminal to shoot him. Of course, why should I worry about shooting him? Just firing over his head will probably give him a heart attack!"

"Boy, you got imagination, just ain't got no faith in me."

"Faith in you, yes! Faith in that buck, no! How come you've never gone before?"

"Went lots of times years ago. Jerry, Peter, me, planned on goin' agin when they got back, a sorta comin' home party. I's workin' on Peter's gun when he died. Was gonna give that gun to Jerry. When they gone, just didn't seem to matter. Didn't have no one special to go with. No one special to share the victory. But now I's goin' back one last time, and you two gonna take me."

"All right, but why is that buck so important?"

"Years ago a piddlin' pile of white trash showed up to work at the turpentine mill. Name was Castle. Didn't take him long to come 'cross me 'cause the Judge often showed his dogs to folks on Sundays. I worked 'em. Castle claimed he'd handled dogs on a chain gang, wanted my job. When he learned his white skin ain't gonna git him my job, he hung my best huntin' hound. Told his crowd he'd done it, too. Thought that'd show Skeeter Hawkins, and that nobody else'd care. Word traveled fast. Folks waited for me to hightail it to the Judge, so he git Castle fired from the mill. But I don't beg for nothin'. I just wait. Sho' 'nough some white kids livin' by the Boggey go in and don't come out. Their pappy come beggin' me to find 'em, but I say I ain't got no dog. He runs to the sheriff, the sheriff gits the Judge, and they all come 'round to my place. It night by this time. The Judge say I can take his best hounds, but I tell 'em I go on one condition: I want Castle with me, unarmed. They don't care. I knowed that. Folks 'round here don't like troublemakers. Don't like things stirred up. Even trash scared ole Castle git them in trouble next."

"But how did you get Castle to go into the Boggey with you?" Steve asked.

"They brung him to me at the Boggey in the police car. He put up a real show, screamin', carryin' on. The sheriff and deputy just draw their .45s, and he decides to go peaceful. Soon he act like he brave, stompin' off in front of me. That last 'til the first snake slither past. Then a tick couldna stuck closer."

"What about the kids?"

"They way back in the Boggey. It's dark as a possum's belly. Dogs had to stay close. Took hours to track. Finally the sun comin' up. I had a notion where them kids was, but first I led ole Castle to this pond fulla quicksand. I raise my gun and orders him to start walkin'. First he thinks I's jokin'. When he seen I's serious, he starts pleadin'. 'Hawkins, don't! Don't shoot me, Hawkins! I ain't done nothin' to you!' "

" 'You hung my dog, Castle!' "

" 'Not me, Hawkins! I swear!' "

" 'You slimy, lyin' excuse for a man. Just keep walkin'.' When he almost to the edge, I order, 'Now turn 'round so you can watch me shoot you, Castle. See, you done run from me, escapin'. You turn to look back, step into the swamp by mistake, and the quicksand git you. Tracks'll show that. Ain't gonna be no tracks from me. If I have to show 'em, it gonna take me a long time to track here. By that time, ain't gonna be much left to pull out.' "

" 'Please, Hawkins! I'll do anything! I'll buy you another dog! Anything, Hawkins!' "

"Now, trash like Castle don't like askin' us for nothin', just like to order us 'round, so I say, 'Feel good, Castle, askin' a nigger to save yo' skin? Like beggin' a nigger to save yo' life?' "

"Now that make him mad. He act like his ole white skin gonna save him. 'They'll never let you git away with this, Hawkins! They ain't never gonna let a nigger kill a white man. Not even you, Hawkins! They'll hang you!' "

" 'Hang me for what? Them white folks don't care if I kill you. They just care it don't *look* like I kill you. Shoot, they gonna love the fact that you died 'cause you careless. Leavin' me, then backin' into quicksand. That'll keep the white folks happy; I been doin' that a long time, Castle.' Then I raise my gun. Castle falls back in the pond, starts tryin' to swim. I sight and git ready for my shot. My finger's on the trigger. Then I heared it —"

"What?" the boys asked.

"A big noise to my right. I turn my head and there he is!"

"Who?"

"The biggest buck I ever seen! His eyes proud and angry. He lookin' right at me, darin' me to fire! Split second all I got. Can't shoot Castle and the buck. I swung my gun to the buck and 'blam!' I know I got that buck, but noise like thunder comin' down on me! Sounds everywhere! Swamp sounds, animal sounds! Never heared nothin' like it since. Next thing I knowed I's flyin' through the air!"

"You mean you missed him?" Steve asked.

"Don't see how, but I did. When my senses back, I's lyin' on the ground with my gun five feet away."

"What do you think happened?" Steve asked.

"Best I can figure, that buck done lowered his head and tossed me with his antlers. I got prints on my stomach, shoulder. But that buck gone! No trace, not even a blood trail."

"But surely you hit him!"

"Thought so, Son. Had my gun right on him not ten feet away."

"If he was comin' fast he could have knocked your gun away!"

"Nope. Had him sighted cold, Son."

"Then you had to hit him even if you didn't kill him."

"What I figure, but no blood. Not then, not later. Nope, that buck a sign I not s'posed to kill nobody, not even a worthless piece of scum like Castle."

"What about him?" Joey asked.

"He 'bout up to his shoulders in the swamp. I pull him out with a limb. He real quiet. Missin' that buck don't mean I ain't gonna still kill him. Later on, he ask why I save him. I tell him he ain't worth killin.' "

"If that buck was real, and if he's still alive, why would you want to kill him?"

"Boy, I been thinkin' on this longer 'n you been breathin'. That ole buck and me gonna meet agin. I searched for him, never found him. Never seen him 'cause it ain't been time. We got unfinished business, and he waitin'. Y'all been talkin' 'bout gittin' a deer since I first knowed you. Now's yo' chance to git a big one. Help me too 'cause I need y'all. Son gonna shoot that buck. Boy, you gonna help me push. We gonna git that ole buck or else."

"Else what?"

"He gonna git me, Son." Skeeter announced calmly as the boys looked at each other, astonished.

"Got yo' permits?"

They nodded.

"Then we go Saturday. Git somebody to work in yo' places 'cause we leave Friday night and camp out. That way we head in at daybreak."

"Skeeter, are you sure the Big Boggey's still there? That's a long way for a mistake."

"Boy, the mistake gonna be takin' yo' blabby mouth chirpin' all the time, 'Where the swamp?' 'This the swamp?' Now, I want to go someplace, and you gonna take me."

The three set off, bumping down country roads. As he gave Joey directions, Skeeter told jokes. When they reached their destination, Joey parked the pickup under a magnolia tree, and Steve helped Skeeter down from the cab. Skeeter walked off toward a row of small, marble gravestones in front of a barbed wire fence in the Oaks Cemetery. When he reached the markers, he took off his battered gray hat and held the brim in silent remembrance for a moment. The boys stood nervously by the truck.

Skeeter looked up and whistled to the boys. "Y'all quit lettin' yo' knees knock and git over here!"

Steve uncrossed his arms and stuffed his hands into his jeans pockets, waiting for Joey to move, but Joey stood biting his lip. Skeeter's laughter only added to their discomfort.

"Git on over here!" he called again, and they slowly walked away from the truck.

"Great white hunters! Think I can't tell you squeamish? I done seen death so many times, I can smell fear. But ain't nothin' to be scared of. You ain't gonna die yet! Ain't nothin' to fear no way if you live right."

The boys tried unsuccessfully to relax.

"Son, come on over here!" he instructed, pointing to his right side. "Boy, you git on this other side, so I can protect you!"

Skeeter placed his hat on the ground in front of him then linked arms with the boys.

"Right where we stand gonna be ole Skeeter. Loretta there with Jerry on the other side." He laughed. "Now why y'all so down in the mouth? Gonna be me under there, not you. Quit bein' scared of my dyin'. This ole man lookin' forward to it."

"Frankly, Skeeter," Steve said, "cemeteries give me the creeps! And I wish you wouldn't talk about dying. It makes me nervous."

"But if you do insist on dying," Joey added, "please don't do it now. We've got all we can handle without having to cart you to the undertaker."

"Don't fret, Boy. I ain't dyin' on you today. Done seen Son's face when he thought I gone. Now, listen to this ole man. When I's restin' here, put a tree at my feet. Make it a tree with fruit for the birds. Do it fast, now, so the birds be singin' over Skeeter soon. Back of this fence put a salt block, so the animals'll come. I want plenty animals and birds keepin' me comp'ny."

The old man's talk slowly relaxed the boys, and the linked arms became a bond. After weeks of a cranky Skeeter Hawkins, Steve and Joey were happy to have their old friend back.

"Skeeter," Joey said. "Maybe we should just cart you to Memphis and bury you under the lions' cage. That way you would have animals over you all the time."

"And plenty of other stuff, too," Steve said, joking.

"Yep, Boy, that another of yo' bad ideas. Now, my instructions in yo' heads?" Skeeter looked from Joey to Steve, and both agreed. Then they stood in a comfortable silence. The lone call of a mockingbird floated across rows of headstones and simple, weather-beaten crosses. A gentle breeze blew the dried summer grass over a green carpet of winter rye. Overhead, like a blessing, was a cloudless blue sky.

"I guess this is a nice place after all," Steve said.

"Yep, real nice place, especially when you ready for it. And today I feel real good! Real good." Skeeter paused, then he startled the boys by singing in a thin, quivering voice, "Dry bones gonna gather in the mornin', come together, and rise and shine. Dry bones gonna gather in the valley, and some of them bones is mine." He let go of the boys' arms, picked up his hat, and strutted off toward the truck, happily singing his song. Joey and Steve could not understand how anyone could be so happy in a cemetery, contemplating his own death. Skeeter stopped, did a few quick steps, and climbed up into the truck. He honked for them, and was still singing his song when they were seated on either side of him. He sang all the way back to the cabin, finally getting them to awkwardly join him on the chorus of the spiritual.

"Would y'all look at that!" Skeeter pointed to the porch

where a black cat sprawled across the floor. "Ole A. Philip Randolph done come back from his travels. Him and me gonna have us some good talks catchin' up."

"Skeeter," Joey said, shaking his head. "You may be a great man with a gun, and you may be able to understand what that mouser says, but you can't sing worth a darn!"

Skeeter poked Joey playfully in the ribs. "You ain't so good neither. Ain't got no rhythm!"

Skeeter laughed at his own joke. The boys were torn between relief that he was happy and confusion over his peculiar behavior. "Y'all know what to bring on this trip. Done had yo'selves a fine teacher. Show up here at five. We eat supper in camp." Then he grew serious. "Son, git inside and take down that .30-30. Practice 'til it a part of yo'self. Boy, git that trap gun of Mr. Manly Broom Dodge. I ain't gonna listen to you yammerin' how Son got somethin' and you don't."

Joey jerked open the pickup door and raced into the cabin. Steve followed more slowly. They had waited months to show off a Skeeter Hawkins gun, and they could not believe Skeeter was loaning them out. All the way back to the truck Joey rubbed the tracing on the metal receiver while Steve cradled the buck like an offering. Skeeter leaned against the blue fender, nodding with pleasure. The boys thanked him again and again, but he waved away their comments.

"Boy, you show up here with yo' muscles twitchin', and this ole man's gonna make you carry a whittlin' knife 'stead of a gun. And I don't want you bringin' that gun on Friday. Carry yo' own shotgun into the Big Boggey."

"When do you want me to bring this back, then, Skeeter?"

Skeeter pulled down his hat and jauntily headed toward the house with his hands in his overall pockets. Without turning back, he loudly announced, "Don't want it agin! Them guns go with y'all now! Dry bones gonna gather in the mornin', come together, and rise and shine. Dry bones gonna gather in the valley, and some of them bones is mine." He continued his song all the way inside the cabin, never once turning around to say good-bye.

"I can't believe this!" Steve said. "I was proud enough he was going to let me use it!"

"*You* can't believe it! I thought he might let you have Jerry's .22, but I didn't think he'd give me a gun, much less this one!" Then Joey grew quiet. "Think we should show them around before we get them insured?"

"I'm not showing this to anyone outside my house until we get back," Steve said. "I'll ask Dad about insurance. Joey, these guns can't be replaced."

Joey stepped closer to Steve and whispered, "Steve, what do you think?"

"I can't believe he gave these to us."

"No, I don't mean the guns. What about this hunting trip? That story happened years ago. That buck's bound to be dead. Do you think Skeeter's losing his mind?"

"I think he's serious about the trip."

"I know that! But what about the rest?"

"Skeeter asked us to take him hunting, and that's what we're going to do," Steve said, pushing any doubts from his mind. "That's all we need to think about."

Twelve

When the boys pulled into the clearing Friday afternoon, Skeeter was waiting on the front porch. A large brown paper sack was his only luggage. He checked the equipment the boys had packed in the truck and noticed a stretcher lying against the side. Steve answered his silent question.

"My dad said we aren't going without that stretcher. With your age and Joey's talent for falling out of trees, he said we'd be lucky if we all got in and out of the swamp in one piece."

"I reckon it go along. But I don't know how this ole man gonna carry two ends of a stretcher when y'all hurt yo'selves."

"Two ends of a stretcher!" Joey said. "You won't be able to carry one end!"

"Watch yo' mouth, Boy, or you find yo'self keepin' comp'ny with the dogs."

"Aren't they going?" Steve asked.

"No. Somebody got to guard this place."

"You're leaving the dogs to guard your guns?"

"Nope, Boy. Orval Faubus guardin' the place, and Abraham Lincoln gonna keep him comp'ny. Don't need no dogs on this trip. Abraham Lincoln a fine huntin' dog, but he can't shoot worth nothin'."

"Skeeter! One dog, even Orval Faubus, isn't much against a determined thief!"

"He be fine. Ole Joe Louis back him up."

"Fine day when you leave your security to a chicken," Joey said climbing into the truck before Skeeter could protest.

"Son, fire off ten bullets. Make sure that rifle workin' with that box. We fire off ten more in the mornin'."

Steve obeyed. When Skeeter was satisfied, the two climbed into the truck beside Joey.

"Boy, you better be glad you in this truck already, else Joe Louis give you a rematch."

"Skeeter, do you want to argue with me about chickens and roosters, or do you want to go hunting?"

"Boy, git this machine movin'!"

Joey followed Skeeter's directions down two country lanes until they reached an old road leading into a tall forest of pine. The truck lurched and bounced all the way to the end of the forest where the landscape opened up into flat land covered with weeds. The boys made camp. After dinner Skeeter spread out a piece of stained tarpaulin.

"That's what you're sleeping on?"

"All I need, Boy. Guess you brung a rollaway."

"We've got sleeping bags."

"Sissy socks," Skeeter muttered as he covered himself with a frayed quilt. "Next you want me tellin' bedtime stories so y'all don't git scared."

"That's a good idea," Steve said. "I like your stories."

"Especially the ones with women," Joey added.

Skeeter laughed, and the pale moon rising overhead and the small crackling fire brought back memories of past hunting trips. The years slipped away, and again he was a young hunter, his voice as natural to the night as the chirping of insects.

"Skeeter," Joey asked during a lull in the stories. "Have you ever been in trouble with the law?"

"Why you ask that, Boy?"

"I just wondered."

"Come close once, at a cockfight."

"A cockfight! So that's why Joe Louis is a killer!"

"Ole Joe Louis never killed nothin'."

"But he could," Steve said.

"Yep. My roosters was the best. Used to fight cocks back in the woods. One night my cock was winnin', but I heared somethin' strange. A sneeze. I look and find Harrison Dodge, the Judge's oldest, and his friend, Freddie Hancock —"

"The lawyer?"

"Yep, Harrison's best friend. They'd hid in the field truck, come with me. So I has to take 'em home. Just on our way when the sheriff drove up. That the closest I come. Told y'all sheriffs used me to track. That partic'lar sheriff and me buddies. Still, I learn early to stay clear of badges."

"What happened that night?" Steve asked.

"Nothin'. We all knowed to keep our mouths shut. Now it time for you mangy dogs to count the stars."

"One, two, three," Joey began as a joke. By the time Joey reached "thirty-five" both Skeeter and Steve were sound asleep.

Orange and violet were streaking the sky when Skeeter kicked the boys awake for breakfast. They both stretched, searching for the dull glimmer of the rising sun, groaned when they realized how early it was, and fell back in their sleeping bags.

"Git up now! Y'all would sleep through a herd of deer stompin' in yo' faces. Some hunters!"

Joey crawled out of his warm lining, but Steve hugged his bag and looked around him. To one side of the camp stood the dark forest of pine and to the other lay the open ground, fringed in the distance by an outline of woods. "Skeeter, are you certain we're at the right place? Does it look familiar?"

"It don't look just like it used to, Son, but I can remember. We drove on some of the old turpentine mill road."

"Some is right!" Joey said. "You're going to have to buy me a new underside for my truck."

"Ain't nothin' to worry 'bout. That truck as ornery as you. Hurry up now with breakfast!"

Steve finished and picked up the .30-30. "Skeeter, where should I fire?"

"Over there, Son. Walk ten feet, fire out in the open, aimin' at that big pine standin' off from the rest. Aim two feet below that last limb. Wake up yo' friend here."

Steve's shots cut through the morning calm.

"Boy, you awake 'nough to find the right end of yo' shotgun?"

"Sure."

"Then git closer to that same tree and fire 'til I say stop."

Joey obeyed and Skeeter nodded in approval. "If y'all re-

163

member what I teached you 'bout trackin' and scoutin', all be fine. If you git lost, use yo' head. Stay put 'til we track back to you. Ain't nobody goin' into the Boggey fidgetin', not payin' attention. That why I teached y'all 'bout flowers and trees."

"Skeeter, where is the Big Boggey? This looks like pasture-land."

"Son, way over yonder as much of the Big Boggey as you gonna want." Skeeter pointed in the direction of the outline of trees in the far distance. "This pastureland gonna git sloppy real soon."

"Skeeter, one question," Joey said. "What are you carrying?"

"Myself. That 'nough for this ole man."

"You're not even carrying a revolver?"

"Why should I? You gonna give me some reason to shoot you, Boy? You and Son armed. These ole bones has all they can do to carry me 'round. Now, come on!"

The three marched across the field, tall grasses rustling against their pants legs. The closer they got to the woods, the soggier the ground became, until pools of water filled the imprints left by their boots. They stopped on the edge of the forest where Skeeter scanned for the best approach. Steve and Joey stood nervously beside him, peering at the thick growth adorned with long, dangling strands of Spanish moss. Skeeter signaled his decision with a brisk nod of his head, and they entered the wooded undergrowth. The air hung over them, thick and dank, smelling of perpetual growth, perpetual death. "Stop!" Joey screamed, shouldering his shotgun. A huge gray snake lay coiled in their path. Steve gasped, but Skeeter was not alarmed.

"It's just an ole moccasin. Walk 'round it. Don't tell the whole place 'bout us on account of one poor snake."

"Poor snake!" Joey said. "It's poisonous!"

"It ain't poisonous 'less it bites you, and it ain't gonna bite you 'less you walk up hollerin' 'Bite me!' Then you git what you deserve, Boy. Now, relax yo' flighty self and come on."

The three stepped gingerly around the moccasin, Joey looking back every step of the way until leaves finally obscured his view. He tried to get Steve's attention, but Steve refused to look at anything except the ground in front of him. Skeeter was pushing limbs and moss out of his way as casually as if he were pushing back bedcovers. After an hour, Joey was still nervous. "Skeeter, where are we heading?"

"To the swamp where I dunked Castle."

"Are you sure it's still there? A lot of this land has been drained."

"Couldn't prove it by this muck," Steve said.

"Boy, quit actin' like a plumber always talkin' 'bout drainin'. Shoulda sent you in here with a wrench 'stead of that shotgun. Now be quiet and pay attention. Open land comin' soon. That ole buck ain't gonna be in this thick stuff 'cause he can't move fast. Just keep payin' attention. Are you markin' yo'self?"

"I'm trying, Skeeter, but this place isn't easy."

"Easy! This is a hunt, Boy. Course, maybe you like yo'self a place with signs, 'This way outta the woods.' 'Stop here to shoot yo'self a deer.'"

Steve laughed while Joey shook his head in disgust.

"Son, you mighty quiet. You trackin'?"

Steve nodded.

"Then tell me where we is."

"We headed south, then turned east when we hit that stream, and walked until we passed that huge cypress with the rotten trunk. When we came around the curve in the water, we angled back southwest. I figure we've walked about a mile since the turn, and the stream's turned with us. I think it should be to our right."

Astonished, Joey asked, "How'd he know that?"

Skeeter gave Joey a stern look. "That right, Boy?"

"Darned if I know."

"Well, Son's right. He know his flowers and trees. You pay attention."

"I am paying attention! I'm looking out for deer, and I don't see any signs. There's no rutting, no scraping, no tracks!"

"Boy, you seen this ole man ruttin' and scrapin'?"

"What?"

"You ain't seen this ole man out scoutin' some lady friend, has you?"

"Who knows, Skeeter," Joey laughed. "Like you once said, you and me talk, but you don't tell me everything."

"Well, I ain't had nothing to tell. That ole buck gittin' too old, just like me, to be spreadin' hisself all over the forest like some young buck. He smart, that how he git old."

"Skeeter, my dad says you're never too old for some things."

"Son, yo' dad a youngun. When he git to be my age, just drawin' his next breath be the only thing in his head. But you go on and look. Soon we be in good deer country. Then you can look for some ruttin'.''

They pushed on, and the boys began to notice a gradual rise in the land. Finally, they emerged in an open area, and Joey looked around and saw what he considered perfect hunting country. Clumps of trees stood here and there, but for the most part, the land was clear. Skeeter ordered the boys to separate and look for evidence. Joey found scraping around a hickory and excitedly called the other two.

"Ain't him," Skeeter said.

"How can you tell?" Joey asked.

"Tracks too small, means young deer. Ruttin' on that oak over yonder too, but too low. Come on. We take another hike and head for the real swamp."

"Oh, Skeeter!" Joey wailed. "We've walked miles!"

"Hush up, Boy! We gonna find him soon."

The solid ground again turned to mush, and they found themselves facing a swamp. Neither boy had to ask where they were, for the place was fearful and frightening. Skeeter pushed back a curtain of moss and disappeared into the forest. Steve followed. Joey swallowed hard, then he too entered the dark, sodden woods. The terrain was the worst they had encountered. Tall trees blocked out the sunlight, and the ground was mud beneath their feet. Ground fog lay in still patches, giving the land a ghostly appearance. They had walked for what seemed an eternity to Joey when Skeeter stopped abruptly and motioned them forward.

"Hand me a stick," he said.

Steve obeyed, and Skeeter moved soggy, brown leaves to

uncover the biggest prints the boys had ever seen.

"There he is," Skeeter said. "Let's go!" They pushed their way through the tangled growth, Skeeter so absorbed in the chase that he seemed to forget their presence. Joey caught up with Steve and grabbed his arm to stop him. "Steve, that can't be the same buck!"

"So what? It's the biggest buck we'll ever see!"

Steve pulled away and hurried to catch up with Skeeter. Joey thought for a moment and decided that it really did not matter if the buck was the same. Steve was right. The prints were the largest he had ever seen. Satisfied, he ran up beside Steve.

"You're right! Who cares? A buck's a buck, and it looks the same to Skeeter."

"Try telling that to Skeeter," Steve said as he pushed himself forward. He wanted to be left alone. He could not talk because he had never told Joey about the eerie sensation he had experienced the first time he looked at the buck on the .30-30. Steve was frightened. Did Skeeter's buck exist, or did the tracks belong to a very old deer? Steve tried to agree with Joey. The buck of Skeeter's memory had to be dead. What did it matter which deer he shot as long as he shot the one Skeeter thought he wanted? One glance at Skeeter answered the question. The man would never be fooled.

The closeness of the timber, the smell of rot, the strange, unfamiliar sounds, all pushed in on Steve, and the picture of the tracks was always one step ahead of him. Their enormous size excited and repelled him.

What if he failed? He brushed aside such doubt with recollections of the long hours on the target range. He would succeed. An animal of that size would be in the record books. If . . . Steve refused to complete the thought. A phantom deer belonged with Santa Claus and the tooth fairy, other childish fancies he had discarded. He shook his head to clear his mind and pushed on after Skeeter.

Their guide kept up the pursuit, stopping occasionally to point out tracks. When he finally stood still to wipe his face, he wore a look of admiration. "That ole buck still smart. He foolin' us 'cause he on to us."

"You mean he knows we're here?" Joey asked.

"Look and tell me what you see."

Steve noticed a rotten log lying across a small rivulet crossing their path. "We've been here before, haven't we, Skeeter? We've crossed that water once."

"Yep, Son. He gittin' us runnin' in circles. Now he headin' for them trees between the pond and open land. Good hidin' place. That ole buck gonna keep far to the right, way outta the reach of that pond, 'cause where I dunked Castle a bad spot. We gonna go straight, right up to the pond and catch up to him."

"How do you know what he'll do, Skeeter?"

"Son, over on yo' left run a stream. That ole buck not gonna take a chance of gittin' slowed down in that water. And he gonna stay clear of that pond up ahead, so he ain't got no way to go but right. Now git goin'!"

Skeeter guided them through marshes and thickets with their boots squishing their muddy release. Joey remembered the sound from childhood when he played in the mud and the rain, but then he had not been scared. Here, without Skeeter, he would be helpless. After pressing forward through a thick cane brake, he moved ahead of Steve to follow directly behind Skeeter. Movement became easier when their feet hit moist packed sand. They were near a large green silt-covered pond. The air was heavy and it stank.

"This place gives me the creeps!" Joey said.

"Go steppin' in that water, you git a taste of what Castle got."

Something plopped in the pond, and circles rippled on the surface. Steve nudged Joey and pointed out a large copper snake disappearing under a log. Joey whispered, "Skeeter."

"Shhh," he softly commanded. "Listen."

A muffled drumming disturbed the thick air.

"You want ruttin', you got ruttin'. He tellin' us he here, back up in them trees!" Skeeter knelt down on one knee and drew a diagram in the sand. "We gonna be a triangle. Son, you the top. But you got to circle 'round that buck. Go east, clear the timber line, follow it north 'til you can head back east. Due north is a big granddaddy oak with a limb lopped off by lightnin'. Stump of that limb yo' perch. When you in place, give the mockin'bird call."

"What if I can't find the tree?"

"Then find somethin' else. If you need to tell us a change, give the hoot owl. Means you comin' back."

"Boy, when Son leave you gonna walk due east 'bout thirty yards. I go west. Stop 'til you hear Son, then answer with the crow. I be the dove. Son know our positions. Then start walkin' northwest. I gonna head northeast. We gonna push that ole buck to Son. That buck gonna have to go forward. When he break the trees, Son, you git him. Make certain you git him on the first shot 'cause he bolt back into the trees."

"Why?" Joey asked.

" 'Cause it easier to git killed out in the open. If he bolt, Son, you holler to Boy that he boltin', and Boy, you git him. More 'n likely, even if Son hit him, he gonna need more 'n one shot."

"What if he bolts your way, Skeeter?"

"Not likely. I be standin' 'tween a stream and a tight line of trees. Won't be much room for him to move. In case he come, I be whittlin' on this stick."

"A stick! What are you going to do with that stick?" Joey asked.

"Slow him down. Once he bolt, you two be runnin' like rabbits comin' to git him."

"Skeeter, I don't believe you," Joey said.

"Ole David done stopped Goliath with a slingshot."

"Skeeter, you don't have a slingshot," Steve said. "We just don't want anything to happen to you."

"You boys do yo' jobs, ain't nothin' gonna happen to me."

"So you're gonna stand there with your stick like a Watusi warrior! I'd feel better if you had a slingshot!"

"Watusi warrior! Boy, you heared that in sickology class? Now that blabby mouth on yo' face got any more questions?"

"No."

"Son?"

"No."

"All right. Remember, don't no one shoot 'less he sees exactly what he's hittin', especially if that buck bolt. Be positive you know everybody's position. Now walk fast. Don't want him to beat us outta the woods."

The boys stood before Skeeter waiting to be dismissed.

They felt as if they had reached graduation; yet, there were no handshakes or murmurings of good luck. All that remained was to give the master teacher the one thing he wanted.

"Git yo' backsides movin'. This Watusi warrior got to git busy on this here stick."

The boys separated, each going his own way into the forest. Joey walked thirty yards, then stopped and waited until the soft mockingbird calls filtered through the trees. Taut with excitement, Joey no longer questioned nor cared about the identity of the buck. He simply wanted a deer. He gave his call and listened as the dove answered him. Then silently, stealthily, he walked through the trees, his every sense sharpened, his fear vanquished. He stopped. Up ahead and to his left he heard movement. He moved on, the sound always ahead of him. Tracks identical to those Skeeter discovered pulled him forward in deadly pursuit of his prey.

Balanced against the trunk of the oak, Steve tried to picture the triangle of Joey and Skeeter coming toward him, and he listened eagerly for sounds of movement. Silence. The deadly calm stifled his initial excitement and nervousness. But a nagging sense of doubt still nestled in the back of his mind. What if he missed? What if he failed Skeeter? Then he heard rustling to the left. Steve leaned forward. The sounds continued, coming closer. Slowly, he lifted the .30-30 and sighted.

Steps came closer, leaves rustled, branches stirred. Then the noises ceased. Steve's heart stopped. He took a breath and continued to sight. Come on, he thought, come on. Suddenly, he felt like someone, something was watching him. He lowered the rifle slowly and peered over the top. He listened. Sounds to his left resumed. There had been no noise on his right. Perhaps Skeeter was watching to see what happened. But then Steve heard the mocking tap of the antlers, and saw him. Antlers filled the air, and the sight of them paralyzed the boy.

Move, you fool! Steve ordered himself. A split second of hesitation was followed by well-practiced movement and he fired. He looked up, and the vacant space screamed at him. He heard the crashing of power through the trees. The buck was bolting right!

"Skeeter, he's coming!" Steve yelled. "Skeeter! Skeeter! He's bolting right!" He jumped down from the oak, almost colliding with Joey as he broke through the woods.

"Did you get him? I thought he was just ahead of me!"

Steve grabbed the front of Joey's hunting jacket, pulling him madly after him. Always the terrible crashing sound was ahead of him, echoing his failure. He stumbled through the trees, still screaming out to Skeeter. A horrible cry pierced the air. The boys ran on until they found Skeeter, bloodied and unconscious in the small clearing near the stream. A sharpened spear was in one hand, a whittling knife in the other.

Steve knelt down, turned the old man over, and cradled him in his arms.

Joey was crying, "Skeeter! Skeeter!" Tears poured down his cheeks. "Skeeter, please be all right! Steve, what are we going to do?"

Steve wiped the blood from Skeeter's shirt and calmly made plans. He barely heard Joey's sobs. They were sounds far beyond him. He knew Skeeter was not dead. He could hear the tortured breathing.

"Joey, shut up!"

Joey stared back at him in shock and disbelief.

"We've got to get him out of here. We can't carry him far by ourselves, so I'm going for the stretcher. You stay here!"

Joey nodded numbly. Steve was shouldering his rifle when Skeeter's raspy voice stilled him.

"Son," he called softly.

Steve knelt beside Skeeter. The man, his eyes filled with weariness, looked up at the boy. "Son, git me home."

Steve nodded. He got up to go, then remembered and looked back at the man on the ground. "Good-bye, Skeeter." Once Steve was out of sight, the teacher closed his eyes.

Joey paced the small area trying to get control of himself. He moved closer and closer to Skeeter until he finally sat down beside him. He could feel the warmth of Skeeter's body through his jeans leg, and took comfort from it. Gradually he began to talk to Skeeter, describing his part in the hunt, recalling past hours together, even telling jokes, anything to drive away his own loneliness. Every few minutes he would sniffle and stop. Once he broke down, sobbing, "Skeeter, please don't leave me! Please don't die!" He felt a soft pat on his leg. Joey leaned down close and whispered, "Skeeter?"

Skeeter slowly, breathlessly spoke. "Come on, Mister Joe. Ain't nothin' to fear. Death and me friends."

"But, Skeeter," Joey protested, "I don't want you to die. What will Steve and I do without you?" Skeeter's lips were still. Afraid to lose Skeeter again, the boy joked, "Why, when will we ever meet another Watusi warrior? I bet you gave that old buck a real scare, standing there with your spear."

Joey did not know exactly what had happened. Determined to find some answers, he got up and searched the small clearing. There was not much to see. Like Skeeter had said, the thick growth of trees obstructed access on one side while the small stream flowed on the other. Skeeter would have had little room to maneuver if the buck had charged through the clearing. He found tracks that disappeared into the forest, but he could not be positive about their age or identity. He found clues, more questions, some answers, but nothing that added up to any more than his own surmises. Frustrated and still frightened, he sat down as close to Skeeter as he could and waited.

Three hours passed before Steve returned with the stretcher. Joey jumped up. "What took you so long?"

"I drove to the nearest service station and called Dad."

"Well, what did he say?"

"They're going to meet us at the truck with the rescue squad —"

"The rescue squad! At the truck! Why didn't you tell him to get that medivac helicopter in here, out in the clearing we came through! They'll take him to Memphis!"

Without looking up, Steve quietly instructed Joey to help get Skeeter on the stretcher. Joey refused to be pacified. "He won't make it if we carry him all the way!"

Steve didn't answer, and Joey gave in to his friend's self-assurance. "All right! So we get him to the rescue squad. What then?"

"They'll radio ahead for Doc Magers. Your dad will bring

him to Skeeter's place. We'll go from there depending on what the doctor says."

"Skeeter's place! He needs a hospital!" The waiting had stripped Joey of his emotional defenses. Now Steve's answers made him feel left out and disregarded.

"I don't understand you, Steve!" he said bitterly.

"Joey, you heard Skeeter. He said to get him home. Now help me get him on the stretcher."

"Did you tell your dad what Skeeter said?"

"Yes."

"What did he say?"

"He said to do what Skeeter asked."

"That means he thinks Skeeter won't make it." Joey's voice broke, and he wiped his nose with the back of his hand.

"Come on, Joey. Let's get going."

The boys placed the unconscious man on the stretcher, shouldered their guns, and picked up their friend. Joey allowed Steve to guide, and he never spoke on the long tramp through the swamp. Steve only gave directions. Skeeter was unconscious but still alive when they came out of the Boggey and sighted the rescue squad waiting for them at the campsite.

Duane Foster put a hand on each boy's shoulder as they watched the rescue team work on Skeeter. Steve's face never lost the blank expression it had worn since he first saw Skeeter lying on the ground. Joey could not raise his head for fear of crying. When the men loaded Skeeter into the white ambulance, Duane Foster instructed Joey to accompany the old man while Steve followed in the truck. Joey got in the ambulance and gave in to his tears.

Thirteen

The rescue squad led the vehicles single file. No sirens sounded. No screeching tires broke the steady pace. Joey felt like he was riding in a funeral procession. He longed to throw open the ambulance door and yell for everything to stop. Instead, he simply stared at Skeeter through a mist of tears.

When the cars pulled up at Skeeter's cabin, the attendants moved Skeeter to his own bed. Abraham Lincoln and Orval Faubus jumped up beside their master and whimpered. Steve patted both of them on their backs. Duane Foster stood at the foot of Skeeter's iron bed talking to the attendants.

Joey could not abide the house. He did not like the two men from the rescue squad eyeing the room's sparse furnishings nor their looks questioning his attachment to the old black man, so he went outside and sat on the worn steps. He did not want to cry, but the sight of his father approaching with Doc Magers triggered the pain welling up inside of him, and he sobbed again. Charles Ryder sat down next to Joey and drew his son to him.

"Dad, he's going to die!"

"Joey, Skeeter's a very old man. Don't you think he's ready?"

"But, Dad, I don't want him to go. He's been one of the best friends I've ever had."

"I know, son, but he's had lots of friends. All of them are gone. His family's dead. If Skeeter had his choice, I don't think he'd want to live."

Joey leaned his head against his father's shoulder. "Dad, it hurts so bad." Charles Ryder handed Joey a handkerchief. "Maybe Steve and I should never have come here. Then I wouldn't feel this way."

"Think of all you would have missed."

"Does it always feel like this when somebody dies?"

"Depends on how you feel about that person."

"Guess Skeeter must have felt this way lots of times. His wife dying, Jerry."

"Old folks have felt lots of pain, usually lots of loneliness. I don't want to live as long as Skeeter unless I have my family around. I couldn't have lived the way he did."

Duane Foster called Charles inside the house. Joey heard the door open, but he did not look up. The two attendants passed him on their way to the ambulance, and he assumed he was alone. Then he heard a familar voice.

"He was a good man, Joey."

"He's —?" Joey asked, startled.

"Not yet, but it won't be long," Doc Magers answered. "There's nothing more I can do. He has heart failure, and one moment his heart will simply stop beating."

"You knew Skeeter, Doc?"

"Not the way some of the old-timers did, but he helped me when I first opened my practice. Most doctors had segregated waiting rooms. I had one empty one, and Skeeter came in one day, looked around, and asked where to sit. When I replied anyplace he liked, he took out a roll of money and peeled off two hundred dollars. I was stunned. No black man in those days usually had that kind of money. Anyway he told me to use the money to treat folks who couldn't pay and to remember that his money was the same color as anyone else's. I called the sheriff the moment he left, and the sheriff told me not to worry. Patients started coming then, mostly poor blacks and whites. Then one day the Judge's black Cadillac pulled up front, and I knew I was officially recognized. I never had to ask for more money because Skeeter always saw to it."

"I wished we'd known you were his doctor. He got real sick one time."

"Joey, Skeeter didn't go to doctors. The only time I treated him was when he got pneumonia, and Fanny Jackson called me out. I thought Skeeter would shoot both of us before I finished examining him. I hadn't seen him for two years until today. I used to stop by when we owned an acreage not far from here. I'm glad I knew him." He patted Joey's shoulder and left.

"Joey," Charles Ryder said from the cabin door. "I'm taking Doc back to town. Duane says he can stay. I can come back, but Steve seems to think the two of you would prefer to be by yourselves."

"We would, Dad."

"Neither of you has ever been through this before."

179

"We'll be all right."

"Duane's taking the truck home and leaving his car in case you need to get us. I'm going over to Fanny Jackson's as soon as I drop off Doc. I imagine she'll want to come over. If we don't hear from you, I'll stop over first thing in the morning."

His father and Duane Foster walked past him on the steps and left. Joey watched until the truck was out of sight and went back inside the cabin. Steve stood staring vacantly out the side window. He did not utter a word or look in Joey's direction. Joey sat down in Skeeter's rocker and listened to the sounds of his own back-and-forth motion until he could stand the silence no longer. "Steve, have you ever seen anyone die?"

"No."

"Neither have I. Are you scared?"

Steve neither answered nor averted his gaze.

"Well, I'm nervous." Joey's words echoed in the cabin's silence. Tears threatened while the face at the window remained still and taut.

The one person who really understood would not even speak. Joey rocked back and forth, his anger at Steve's distance building. Finally, unable to stand the silence and rejection, Joey stalked from the room, slamming the screen door.

The hours dragged by. Skeeter showed no change in his condition and appeared to be sleeping peacefully. Now and again, Joey sat on the bed beside his old friend. He also tried unsuccessfully to nap on the floor. When he grew tired of resting, he paced the room or walked around the property.

Finally, around eight o'clock he sat down on the front steps to wait, but the sound of an approaching car interrupted his vigil. An unfamiliar green-and-white Ford drove into the clearing. A car door opened and someone got out. The car then moved away, leaving a motionless figure standing in the light from the cabin's door. The visitor was a tiny, gray-haired woman with a tight bun at the nape of her neck. She clasped a cane, and her diminutive size and age made him feel protective. Rising from the steps, he hurried over to help.

"You must be Boy. Skeeter told me all about y'all. He said you'd growed into a tall drink of water, but you still had a right pretty baby face."

"That sounds like Skeeter. You must be Mrs. Jackson. Here, let me help you," Joey said taking her arm.

"Yo' daddy offer to bring me out earlier, but I waited 'til my neighbor could come. My daughter, Shirley, works nights at the hospital. Skeeter the same, I reckon?"

"Yes, ma'am. He hasn't regained consciousness. Guess this really isn't the time, Mrs. Jackson, but I want to thank you for my basket. Skeeter said he gave you my note."

"Yes, he did. And I thank you, Boy. Nobody 'round to make me splits. Sure enjoyed them you did."

"Oh, it was good for me. I didn't like it at the time, but it taught me everything doesn't have to come from the store. My mom and I fight over the basket now. She puts it in the den, and I take it back to my room."

"We see to that, Boy. I got splits for one last basket. I make it for yo' mama."

"She'd really like that."

Joey stopped at the steps. Steve had never wavered in his

watch by the window, and Joey was embarrassed. "My friend Steve's inside the house —"

"Son? I sho' be glad to meet him. Been lookin' forward to meetin' both you boys."

"He's acting a little dumb. He's hardly talking. He just stands at the window."

"Don't worry none. I been 'round lots of boys."

The two entered the house. After first glancing in the direction of Skeeter, Mrs. Jackson looked at Steve. She paused as if considering the greatest need, then moved toward the figure at the window and extended her hand. "You must be Son." Steve turned and awkwardly shook hands.

"I hope you boys don't mind me callin' you Son and Boy. That's what I always heared Skeeter say. Yep, Skeeter took quite a shine to you boys. Not just any younguns spend time with old folks like us."

She walked over to the bed and looked down at Skeeter. She gently touched his forehead, then each cheek, before turning back to the boys.

"Boy, if you'll take my coat, I'll fix some supper. Bet y'all are hungry."

Despite Joey's protests, Fanny Jackson began frying potatoes and opening pork and beans. Soon the smells of food filled the small cabin. The boys had not realized how hungry they were. While they ate, Fanny Jackson sat on Skeeter's bed, stroking his arm and talking softly to him. The old man did not respond, but her gentle tones brightened the room.

"Boy, you seen Skeeter's album?" she asked after the dishes had been put away.

"No, ma'am."

"Just like him. Never had no time for photos, but Loretta left some in a box. We had plenty. My daughter, Shirley, put some in a album for him one Christmas. Thought he might like to look at them. Hard to find somethin' to give Skeeter. Check behind his clothes over there and look under the bed. It's here someplace."

While Steve returned to his vigil at the window, Joey pulled a thick green album from under the bed and sat next to Mrs. Jackson. Jerry, Loretta, the Judge, Harrison, and Peter all stared out at him, no longer simply characters in an elderly man's humorous stories, and the boy realized with some pain that as much as he loved Skeeter Hawkins, the man had never really belonged to them. Page after page revealed Skeeter's past, and Joey saw what a tiny segment of his friend's life he and Steve had shared.

"Mrs. Jackson," Joey asked as she closed the book. "Do you think Skeeter was peculiar? Some people said he was."

"Them folks white?"

"Yes, ma'am."

"Mm-hmm. Colored folks havin' pride used to make whites nervous. They'd say we's gittin' uppity, and gittin' uppity got colored folks in lots of trouble. But Skeeter couldna been a cropper sayin' 'yessir' all the time. Somebody woulda gotten killed, that somebody woulda been white, and Skeeter woulda been strung up. He knowed that, so he set out to make his own way, the only way he knowed. That was bein' the best at what he do. Now everybody 'round here know Skeeter can shoot and track. They need him. Can git another cropper; can't git another Skeeter. But Skeeter keeped his pride. White folks can't admit they's got a proud colored man walkin'

183

'round. So the white folks just say Skeeter was peculiar. And Skeeter didn't walk in front of folks much. He just took his prideful self out into the woods. That way everybody satisfied. Understand? That was a long time ago for a youngun like you."

"I guess. Is that why he moved out here by himself?"

"Not really. Skeeter always had the woods to hide in. He come out here after everybody gone. He coulda stayed in town with us. He wanted peace and quiet. Folks always badgerin' him in town, wantin' him to fix this, watch them shoot. Skeeter didn't want the world beatin' a path to his door, so he just moved the door."

"Didn't you worry about him?"

"Worry about Skeeter Hawkins? Land sakes, child, no one woulda wanted to face the end of Skeeter Hawkins's gun."

"Do you think he was lonely?"

"All old folks git lonely, Boy, but you need to remember, Skeeter spent his life in the woods because that's the way he like it. And he isn't alone. He has his animals, me, you, Son. And with Loretta's help, Skeeter became a believer. Believin' folks ain't never really alone. Skeeter has some life to look back on, some life." Smiling, she looked out into space and back into time.

"Soon, I'll be the only one left. Not that we see each other all that much, but it's nice to know the other can come if need be. Now, talkin' has tired me out. You tell me all about you and Son over there."

The long silent hours with Steve and Skeeter had taken their toll, and Joey found himself talking about everything that came to mind. He discussed his family, school, his plans, his friendship with Steve, and their time with Skeeter. Fanny Jackson sat quietly, occasionally asking a question. Finally, Joey could think of no more to say.

"Well, I guess that's it. I hope I didn't bore you too much."

"No, child. I enjoy hearin' 'bout young folks. Now tell me all the news of this huntin' trip the three of you was on. Skeeter told me you two was takin' him. Was he excited! I ain't seen him so happy in years."

No tone of recrimination edged her words. No sorrow, no bitterness flowed through her voice, so Joey felt safe telling her what happened from the moment he and Steve loaded up in town. The more he talked, the more he discovered how much he needed to talk about the trip. He filled in every detail, laughing where Skeeter laughed, telling the old man's stories and describing the land they crossed.

"Then we fanned out. I was on the east side of the triangle walking northwest on the diagonal. And at first, was I nervous! Then I calmed down and got real steady. Skeeter was supposed to be coming northeast on the diagonal. We were trying to force the buck toward the oak at the top of the triangle the three of us formed with our starting positions. That way, he would walk right out to where Steve was sighting. I got to where I could hear the buck! He was right ahead of me and to my left! Shoot, for a time I thought I might ram right up on top of him! Then I heard a shot! Then a crashing noise off to my left! See, Steve missed . . ."

The door slammed. "Steve missed. Steve missed," Joey repeated until at last he understood.

"That boy not bein' dumb," Fanny Jackson said softly. "That child hurtin' bad."

"Should I go after him?"

"No, leave him be."

Joey and Mrs. Jackson talked until past midnight when she asked him to take her home. Reluctantly he agreed. He dreaded the silent cabin with or without Steve. He feared being alone with Skeeter if he died, but he would not admit this by begging the woman to stay. He went to get her blue coat while Mrs. Jackson stood beside Skeeter. Joey did not mean to eavesdrop, but her words were unmistakable.

"Loretta always say she has to wait on you, Skeeter. Well, old man, Loretta been waitin' on you a long time now. Like my Henry. He been waitin' twelve long years. Time old folks like us stopped all this foolishness and got where we're headin'." She leaned over and kissed his forehead.

"I be back first thing in the mornin'," she said to Joey. "Can't stay here with y'all. Be too hard on me with what's comin' up to do. My daughter Shirley don't have to work tomorrow, so we be out."

"Mrs. Jackson," Joey said. "This is a bit embarrassing for me, but would you do something?"

"Sure, child. What is it?"

Joey held out the small wooden dog he had carved. "If . . . when the time comes, would you see that this dog goes with Skeeter? It would mean a lot to me since I carved it for him."

"Of course, Boy. Skeeter would like that."

"I heard that the Egyptians buried their dead with carvings of people and animals to protect them on their way. I think Skeeter would like to have a dog along to keep . . ." His voice broke and he swallowed. Fanny Jackson put her arms around him. "Now, child, everythin' gonna be all right. You gonna be fine 'cause Skeeter just goin' on a trip. We gonna say good-bye here. Folks gonna meet him at his destination. And they're gonna be real happy to see him. Just you remember that. Now, come on. Help me down them front steps."

Joey felt better as he helped her out of the cabin and down the steps. "Steve!" Joey called out into the darkness. "I'm taking Mrs. Jackson home." No one answered.

"Head me around back, child. Then leave me be."

Joey suspected that she was looking for Steve, but did not ask. At the back of the house, she let go of his arm and headed slowly toward the tool shed. The moon cast eerie shadows, and Joey worried that Mrs. Jackson might trip and fall. Her steps, however, were steady.

Fanny Jackson found Steve hunched over with his head resting against his knees. She took a long look in the faint light, then, leaning forward on her cane, she spoke gently but firmly. "We carry 'round a load of guilt in this life, child. Most of it we carry rightly 'cause it belong to us. What don't rightly be ours we need to git rid of 'cause it too heavy a load. Love, now that light enough to carry 'round extra, and we need to carry extra 'cause love keeps us goin' in this life. Whatever happened out there, you got no cause for blamin' yo'self. There a time for everything. Like the Good Book say, there a time to be born and a time to die, especially for old folks to die. Skeeter, why he lucky. He gonna die in his own bed after one last huntin' trip. Wished I could choose my time, my way. Son, Skeeter would be hurtin' bad if he knowed what a burden you carryin'."

She paused and watched as the boy turned his head toward her. She could not see his face, but knowing that he could not speak, she continued. "Skeeter was real proud of you, Son. He say you gonna be as good a shot as Jerry, and Jerry the best shot Skeeter Hawkins could train. But Jerry was quiet, carried 'round more inside of him than he ought. Used to tear him up the way things was. He'd bang his head 'ginst that old white wall, git so mad at the way things was, git so frustrated 'cause he couldn't do some things. Not always easy bein' Skeeter Hawkins's son, neither. Skeeter could usually find his way 'round problems. Jerry was young. He refuse to try. When he growed up, he started feelin' guilty. One time him and my girl, Shirley, was downtown, and some white boys made nasty remarks to her. Jerry wanted to stop and fight, but Shirley kept walkin'. She reminded him that Skeeter told Jerry not to fight 'less he was ready to lose it all; then the fight better be worth takin' on. That time Jerry say if he'd been tough enough them white boys woulda been so scared they'd never said them things to Shirley. He blamed hisself for their nasty mouths. Claimed they'd never said that stuff if Skeeter had been there. Got to where he blamed hisself for everything that grieved him. Then he went away to the war and never come back. War killed him, but guilt drove him away, guilt and anger at the way things was. Skeeter never got over it. Blamed hisself. Grieved more for that boy when things start to changin' 'cause he don't have no son, no grandson, no great-grandson, to breathe free. Skeeter spent too much of his livin' feelin' guilty. Don't burden his dyin' with yo' guilt, child. Let the old man lie easy."

Fanny Jackson turned and walked slowly away. Joey was waiting for her by the porch. "That child gonna break in two if he don't git it out."

Joey took Mrs. Jackson into town, then drove back slowly in order to prolong the trip. When he entered the cabin, Steve was sitting in the rocker. The dogs had not moved from the bed.

"Steve."

The boy did not look up at him.

"Steve, it wasn't your fault. So you missed. It probably wasn't even the same bu ——"

"Shut up, Joey! Just shut up!"

"All right. All right," Joey said. "Let's trade off. You want to nap first?"

"No!"

"I'm going to lie down. Wake me if you need me."

Joey stretched out on the floor. He missed Mrs. Jackson and thought about the things she had said. Gradually the long hours came over him, and he dozed off. Around sunrise Steve shook him awake. Fear gripped Joey, and he quickly got up.

Steve stood on one side of the iron bed, Joey stood on the other. It did not last long. The final sounds, then release.

Joey immediately left the house. The sun was almost up in the sky. He went around to the shed, sat on the stoop, and cried. He got up and went to the pond, walked to the creek, and stopped in all the important spots in the clearing, listening to the old man's voice, pulling memories to himself. He had to make this last visit before returning to the cabin to accept the reality of Skeeter's death.

When he did return, Steve was still standing by the bed. He looked at Joey and solemnly announced, "They're gone."

"What are you talking about?"

"The guns. They're gone. I went to get them —"

"Why?"

"I wanted to put them back on the wall. I wanted things back to the way they're supposed to be. I want things back to the way they should be."

Fourteen

The boys sat uncomfortably in Fred Hancock's office. Since Skeeter's death, Steve and Joey had busied themselves with self-appointed tasks that they did not like interrupted, especially when their fathers refused to tell them the purpose of coming to the lawyer's office or to show any concern over the missing guns. Neither boy had ever visited a lawyer, and Hancock's entrance did nothing to relieve their uneasiness. An older man with neatly trimmed white hair, Hancock wore a smartly tailored three-piece charcoal gray suit and expensive jewelry.

"I want to thank you for coming down," Hancock said. "You're probably wondering why you're here, so I'll tell you right off that Skeeter requested it."

Surprised, both boys looked up.

"Skeeter came in last week with your dads —"

"He sent Abraham Lincoln over to the Ryders' last week with a note while you were at work," Duane Foster interrupted to explain. "He asked Charles and me to come over. He didn't want you boys to know."

"Skeeter had some things that he wanted done after he passed away and asked me to see to it. I've handled his legal business for years. To be honest, I'm not certain I understand all of his directions, and I've known him all my life."

"He told us about the time you and Harrison Dodge snuck out to the cockfight," Joey said.

"He did! We spent all our growing-up days at Skeeter's heels. He taught me to shoot, taught my son to shoot." Fred Hancock began pulling papers from a file. "Skeeter assured me that you would understand what he wanted. The tasks are mostly odds and ends. Skeeter outlined what to do with the bulk of his estate several years ago. Skeeter was not a rich man, but he did well for his time. The Dodges helped him buy land. The Judge's brother, Manly Broom Dodge, left him the land on which the cabin sits, and the Judge left him black rental properties. Skeeter sold off his farms several years ago to his good tenants. The proceeds of those sales go to a scholarship fund at the high school for black students. The money from the remaining rental property goes to Fanny Jackson, then to her daughter, Shirley. At Shirley's death, the properties will be sold and the proceeds revert to the scholarship fund. Now, you boys come in at this point." He looked down at his notes.

"Skeeter said that Fanny Jackson will see to his burial, but you boys are to take care of the tree and the salt block for his grave. You understand that, I assume?"

"Yes, sir," Joey answered.

"Then you are to take care of the animals. The chickens go to Fanny Jackson, and you are to tell her about Joe Louis. The remaining animals can go where you boys see fit, except for the mule, Franklin D. Roosevelt. Steve is to put him down with a single shot from his .30-30, and he is to be buried in his corral. Is that agreeable with you, Steve? Skeeter said you would know which gun to use."

Steve nodded. Hancock noticed the boy grit his teeth, but did not ask any questions.

"Now to the rest of the animals: Abraham Lincoln, Orval Faubus, A. Philip Randolph, Trouble, Martin Luther King, Jr., Sex Kitten, and Tammy Northcutt." Fred Hancock paused. "How did he let the name Northcutt get on that list, unless it's a rattlesnake?"

"The last three are kittens who belong to A. Philip Randolph and Trouble," Joey answered. "We were naming the kittens one afternoon. Steve's been dating Tammy Northcutt. We didn't know Skeeter had such a thing against her family —"

"Thing! He damned near killed Sam Northcutt, Tammy's grandfather. The night Loretta died was the only time I ever saw Skeeter lose control. He blamed Northcutt for letting Loretta die, and he threatened to kill him right in the hospital. Sam swore he didn't realize how bad off Loretta was, but Skeeter became a madman. It took the sheriff, the Judge, and me to get him home and that was the easy part. Keeping him there was what was hard. The Judge and the minister from the Mount Moriah Baptist Church took turns with some of the rest of us for four days watching him. But the Judge knew what Skeeter was feeling. His own wife was dead, and they had both lost their sons. They were two old broken men, keeping each other sane. But I'm getting off the track. I was surprised when Skeeter mentioned the name, but

I didn't want to question him, knowing how he felt about Northcutt."

Joey nodded, remembering Skeeter's one explosion.

"When you finish with the animals, you may move the tool shed or destroy it. The contents are yours. Fanny Jackson will take what she wants from the cabin. Once everything is cleared away, he wants the two of you to burn the corral, cabins, and outbuildings. Everything is to be destroyed within a week after the funeral."

"Why?" Joey asked. "Why did he want it all burned?"

"Skeeter said that when he's gone, he's gone. The land goes to the county for a conservation or recreation area, and the county would burn the place anyway, so he wanted it done by someone he trusted. He wants it done quickly, so you boys can get on with your lives. Once you have completed all this, come back down and we'll go over the collection. The estate will see to the appraisal and insurance. For the appraisal, I will need the shotgun back from you, Joey, and the .30-30 after Steve takes care of the mule. I don't need to tell you how valuable Skeeter's guns are."

"I don't understand, Mr. Hancock," Joey said.

"I assumed you knew. Skeeter left the guns to you boys."

"Excuse me, please," Steve said quietly. He left the room. Duane Foster followed and found Steve leaning against a wall in the corridor.

"Son, are you all right?"

Steve nodded.

"Steve, I need to talk to you about all of this."

"Not now, Dad, please."

"You've got to deal with this thing."

"I can't, Dad. Not now, I can't."

Steve and his father returned to Hancock's private office where the lawyer continued. "Skeeter said you would understand that you are never to sell the exceptional guns and would know how to pass on the collection. The bits and pieces in the tool shed and some of his common guns may be sold." Hancock looked steadily at each boy. "I have lists for you. Basically the shotguns go to Joey and the rifles to Steve."

The boys took the lists. Joey was pleased to see that he had the old shotgun Skeeter had taken off the moonshiner. He knew Steve had Jerry's .22, and he elbowed him to get a reaction, but Steve was not even looking at his list.

"Do you boys have any questions?"

"No, sir," Joey answered. "I just hope we can do it like Skeeter wanted."

"I'm sure you will." Hancock stood up and said, "I do have a question I've been wanting to ask."

"Go ahead."

"I was just interested in how you two and Skeeter —"

"Got to be friends?" Joey finished.

Hancock nodded.

"We were the ones who were sent. Skeeter knew it the first time he met us, and we spent a lot of time with him. It really doesn't make sense to anyone but us and Skeeter."

"Obviously it meant something to Skeeter, and that's what counts. I'm glad to meet you two. Thanks for coming down." He extended his hand.

The boys arrived with their parents at the Mount Moriah Baptist Church. Joey nodded to Doc Magers and noticed several other men in the country club set. He did not recognize a handsome, thickset man with salt-and-pepper hair sitting next to Fred Hancock, but Joey guessed the man was Harrison Dodge. The boys sat down and stared at the hymnals on back of the pews, suspicious that everyone present was looking at them. They imagined that the whites were staring because they had inherited Skeeter's guns, and they suspected the blacks were questioning why they were there.

When the service began, Steve and Joey felt as if they had walked into the funeral of a stranger. The minister obviously did not know Skeeter well, and they listened as he quoted scripture, talked abstractly about death, and catalogued Skeeter's charitable acts to the community. Only when the choir sang a rousing version of "Dry Bones Gonna Gather in the Mornin'" did the boys feel in touch with Skeeter.

The service at the cemetery was equally uncomfortable. A scalloped blue canopy, metal chairs for Fanny Jackson and her family, and banks of flowers all seemed an ugly invasion of Skeeter's private territory. Each boy remembered Skeeter's hat resting where the casket stood. They listened to the minister's graveside remarks and paid their respects to Fanny Jackson. Her hugs assured them that they were an important part of the funeral.

They were standing off to the side awkwardly when Hancock and another man approached.

"Boys," Fred Hancock said. "I have someone who'd like to meet you." The handsome stranger stood in front of them. "Harrison Dodge, Steve Foster and Joey Ryder." The man's handshake was firm, and Joey noted an air of commanding self-assurance which made him uneasy. Although Dodge had an open, accepting look on his face, Joey was suspicious that the visitor would question how he and Steve came to inherit Skeeter's guns. When the man spoke, his words confirmed Joey's fear.

"There are many people I know who are very envious of you boys. Skeeter was badgered for years about his guns. He never would say what he was going to do with them." Joey decided that he disliked the man intensely, and Steve was grinding his teeth. But then Harrison Dodge said something that caught their attention. "But don't let his giving you those guns bother you. I've known Skeeter Hawkins all of my life, and I know he wouldn't leave that collection to someone who didn't measure up. Skeeter had very high standards. Believe me, I know. I have my dad's collection of guns carved by Skeeter, and I have the ones Skeeter carved for me personally. Fred also has guns Skeeter did for him. We could sell them any day for thousands of dollars. But as far as we're concerned, they're without market value because they're irreplaceable. So you hang on to that collection. Skeeter gave them to you for a reason, so be proud of them and be proud of yourselves for getting them."

Relieved and grateful, Joey confessed, "Thanks, Mr. Dodge. We were excited to get the guns."

Steve remained silent.

"I'm glad Skeeter was out hunting at the end," Dodge continued. "That's the way he would have wanted it. And I'm glad he was with you boys. Skeeter always enjoyed boys. You know he raised a son, Jerry? That's his grave next to Loretta's."

"Skeeter told us about him and about your brother, Peter."

"Which one of you has Jerry's .22?"

"I do," Steve answered softly.

Harrison Dodge looked at the quiet boy and knew not to press.

"Skeeter told us that you have Peter's," Joey said.

"My son does. Soon my grandson will. I still have the .30-30 he began carving as a welcome home present for Peter. He never finished it. I guess he told you that Peter was killed in the Korean War."

"Yes, he did."

Harrison Dodge turned and stared solemnly at Jerry's headstone. "My dad never got over Peter's death, and Skeeter never got over Jerry's. It's sad to wish a violent death on someone, but I think it would have been easier for Skeeter if Jerry had been shot."

"You mean he wasn't?" Joey asked. "He told us that Jerry was killed in the war."

"He was, but he drowned. Peter was killed in action."

"How could he drown?"

"He couldn't swim, or at least he couldn't swim very well. It's easy to drown when you're crossing a swiftly moving river with heavy equipment on your back." Harrison Dodge looked over at Fred Hancock in anticipation of leaving, but Joey could not drop the subject. There was something he did not understand.

"But how could a son of Skeeter's not be a good swimmer?"

"I don't know that Skeeter knew how to swim."

"Why not? He knew how to do everything else out of

doors. He went into swamps, all sorts of places with water."
Joey looked at the men and sensed they were uncomfortable.

"He didn't have a real place to learn. There wasn't a public pool here until the early fifties, and it was segregated. Cow ponds and creeks were all that was available to the black community."

"Oh," Joey murmured, his one word conveying a world of realization.

"Jerry, then Peter, Loretta, my dad. Skeeter was alone. I'm glad he took up with you two boys. Funny things about those boys though. They grow up to look like me, Fred, and the rest of these wrinkled, old men you see standing around here." Harrison Dodge smiled and held out his hand again. "Take care."

"Thanks, Mr. Dodge. If you're ever back in town and have some time, we'd love to hear stories about Skeeter."

"Be glad to tell you, but you don't have to wait for me. Fred has almost as many as I do."

"Sure. Come on down, and we'll talk. A man my age never passes up a chance to reminisce, especially to a willing audience."

"Thanks, Mr. Hancock. Good-bye, Mr. Dodge."

"Good-bye."

"Come on, Joey. Let's go," Steve said pulling on his tie. "I can't wait to get out of here and change my clothes."

"Well, I thought I'd speak to Mrs. Jackson and maybe meet some of her family first."

Joey was not anxious to leave because he did not look forward to spending the afternoon with Steve. He knew Steve was having a hard time with Skeeter's death, but he didn't know how to help him. Steve didn't seem to want to be helped.

Steve walked away, so Joey said, "All right. Let's go. I'll be back at your house in an hour."

On their way to the cemetery, they stopped by the cabin and picked up Abraham Lincoln and Orval Faubus. At the freshly covered plot, the animals lay down on the flowers covering their master. Orval Faubus whimpered. The dogs stayed on Skeeter's grave the entire time the boys planted the mulberry and positioned the salt block. But as the boys replaced the shovels in the truck, Abraham Lincoln walked over to Steve and barked twice. The dog sat on his haunches and looked up sorrowfully at the boy.

"Guess he's made his decision," Joey said. "I'd sure like to have him, but Skeeter always said that you and he were the same type. Besides, I've got Jackie Robinson. You're going to take him, aren't you?"

"Sure." Steve knelt down and put his arms around the black-and-white dog. "Good boy. Come on, let's go home." When Steve opened the truck's door, the dog jumped up in the front seat.

"What are we going to do with him?" Joey asked, looking back at the white hound. Orval Faubus was still lying listlessly across the flower-strewn mound.

"Try and get him to leave. If not, we'll leave him here. We'll be back."

"How's he going to eat?"

"He hasn't since Skeeter died. Maybe he'll make his own decision about what's going to happen to him."

The boys brought a sack of dry dog food back from the cabin, but they could not cajole Orval Faubus into eating or moving from the grave. Finally they left him some food and gave up for the afternoon.

All the way back to town Steve sat with his arm draped around Abraham Lincoln while he helped Joey plan the next two days. Joey was relieved that Steve was acting more like his old self, and he knew that the dog was the reason.

The next morning the boys tossed for the pipe and Skeeter's Mason jar, both of which Fanny Jackson had left behind in the cabin. They moved the chickens to her house, and Joey gave Joe Louis a few minutes of stroking before releasing him in his new home. A. Philip Randolph objected strenuously to being driven anywhere in the truck and showed his disdain for the Ryders' barn by returning to Skeeter's cabin steps after lunch and racing away whenever the boys approached. Once they finished the animals, they loaded up the boat and returned it to the Fosters'. Then they packed up the shed. Finally, they waited for Duane Foster to appear with the .30-30, and when he did, Steve felt sick.

Steve approached Franklin D. Roosevelt's corral telling himself that it was simply a matter of putting a dumb animal out of his misery. Skeeter had asked him to do it, and he was actually doing Franklin D. Roosevelt a favor. The mule would feel nothing. He would feel nothing, Steve almost convinced himself as he stepped through the corral gate and raised his rifle. He aimed. The animal looked up at him, and Steve lowered his rifle. Steve took a deep breath and raised the rifle again. He started to squeeze the trigger, keeping his eyes focused on the mule's head, but the face staring back at him was not that of a dumb animal. Steve squinted and aimed again. Skeeter was looking back at him. Steve looked up and saw Franklin D. Roosevelt. He aimed and saw Skeeter. Steve felt something hot slide down his face, and his stomach tightened into a knot. He tried to sight again but knew that for a second time he was a failure. Steve let the rifle slide to the ground. He ran blindly through the woods to the pond where he threw himself on the grass. His sobs were foreign and sickening to him. Steve cried until he heard his father's voice.

"Steve," Duane Foster said. "I've talked to Joey. Skeeter's death was not your fault."

"Yes it was, Dad. I missed the buck, and he got Skeeter!"

"You don't know that."

"Yes I do! I saw the buck! It was the same one, the one Skeeter wanted me to kill!"

"Steve, you saw a buck, or you think you did —"

"I saw him!"

"All right, you saw him. That doesn't make Skeeter's death your fault."

"Yes it does. Skeeter said that if we did our jobs, nothing would happen to him. Now he's dead!"

"Steve, sit up and let's talk."

Steve obeyed, trying to control his tears. He took the handkerchief his father offered, but he refused to face him.

"Steve, why do you think Skeeter wanted to go on that hunt?"

"To kill the buck. He told us, Dad."

"That's what he told you. Maybe even he thought that's

what he wanted to do, but Skeeter didn't expect to come out of the Boggey alive."

Steve looked around at his father in sickened disbelief.

"Why do you think I made you put that stretcher in the truck? I didn't put it in there for Joey. I made you take it for Skeeter, and he didn't make you take it out."

"He told you he wanted to die?"

"Of course not. But why else would he ask us to help him get his things in order? He had everything taken care of by Friday, even got the guns out of the cabin and down to Fred Hancock. Does that sound like a man who's planning on living? He knew he was failing, and he didn't want to linger, dying a little at a time. If you ask me, it's a great way to go."

"But the buck. I saw him!"

"You saw him! Maybe even Skeeter saw him! There are all sorts of things that could have happened! According to Doc, Skeeter died of heart failure, an old man's death. Sure the buck could have caused it. If he bolted through that narrow passage where Skeeter stood, and I say *if*, he could have scared Skeeter to death."

"The marks! Skeeter had marks! Skeeter was bloody!"

"Joey said he searched the spot for evidence. Skeeter was carving on a stick. He might have fallen on his own stick or even his own whittling knife. But Steve, it doesn't matter. Don't you see? Even if the buck had killed Skeeter, even if he had gored him to death, that's what he wanted. It doesn't matter that you missed."

"Yes it does!" Steve screamed. "It matters to me! I failed Skeeter! He trained me to be good enough, and I wasn't! I missed, so I failed him! He could have died of excitement! He could have died on the way out of the Boggey! He could have died if I shot the buck, but he didn't! He died because I missed the buck. I failed Skeeter and he died!"

"Steve, he trained you for the same reason all men pass what they have to who they have. He told Charles and me that he had hoped to keep the guns in the family, but there was nobody close by who measured up. You did. He gave you the things he had, and those guns are a wonderful gift, because you valued the things he valued most, his knowledge and his skill. Can't you try to understand that? For your sake and Skeeter's?"

"But you still don't understand, Dad. He gave me that rifle to take into the Big Boggey!"

"That's one reason he gave you the rifle, but it's certainly not the most important reason. He gave you the rifle because you deserved it. He wanted you to have it, and he wanted you to use it. Don't you realize what happened back at the corral?"

"Yes! I can't even shoot a poor, sick, old mule!"

"Yes you can, because that's another reason Skeeter gave you the rifle. That was among his last requests to you."

"You don't think Skeeter cared about the buck?"

"I imagine he did, but he also just wanted to make that one last hunting trip. If he died during it, so much the better. And I do know that he cared about that mule. Do you want Franklin D. Roosevelt to suffer?"

"No."

"Do you want some vet to shoot him like it's all in a day's work?"

"No."

"I can call Doc Haskell, and that's exactly what he'll do with an animal that size. Then you will have failed Skeeter. Now get out there and do what you have to do!"

Steve nodded. Duane Foster squeezed his son's shoulder and left. Steve looked out over the still pond, scene of so many happy memories.

He remembered the first time he had seen the gun stock and knew there was a buck. Then he thought back to the afternoon when Skeeter had told him about the deer. Skeeter himself had missed. Maybe his father was right. If Skeeter had been determined for Steve to make that one perfect shot, he would have been there and torn Steve apart, movement by motion, and they would have gone again. Again, Steve promised himself, I'm going again.

Steve walked back to the clearing. He did not feel any better about killing Franklin D. Roosevelt because he loved the old mule. So had Skeeter. The .30-30 still lay on the ground. Steve picked it up, feeling as if he were holding a year of his life in his hands. He stood for a moment, knowing that he would give back the gun and his entire collection if he could only return to Skeeter and the boy who now seemed a stranger in his past. Steve moved to where Franklin D. Roosevelt stood placidly in the corral and sighted. He pulled the trigger and cried.

The boys buried Franklin D. Roosevelt in his corral, and Joey placed a hay wreath on the grave. Neither knew what to do next.

"We've got to do something else," Joey said.

"Like what?"

"Sing, pray, say something."

"I pass, Ryder."

"Can you whistle? Listen." Joey began whistling "Dry Bones Gonna Gather in the Mornin'," and Steve joined in on the chorus.

"Guess that business about bones rising goes for mules too," Joey said when they finished.

"Ryder, sometimes I wonder about you! Come on, let's go see about Orval Faubus at the cemetery."

The boys had no luck with the old dog. He would hardly admit their presence. Joey tried to pick him up, but Orval Faubus bared his teeth and snapped at him, so he gave up. They put more dried food next to their earlier untouched offerings and went home, holding out little hope that the dog would survive.

The next day the boys faced their tasks with dread. They could not imagine destroying the cabin, the corral, the tool shed, all a part of Skeeter. When they reached the clearing, they walked over the entire area several times searching for anything that might have been overlooked.

When they were satisfied that nothing remained, they pulled away brush according to the fire chief's instructions. They tried to find A. Philip Randolph, but the old mouser had disappeared. There was nothing more to do until the fire department truck arrived, so the boys sat down on the steps to talk. They had thought they would want to prolong every moment with what was left of Skeeter, but without the lively presence of Skeeter himself they saw only ramshackle buildings. They preferred their memories and were eager to finish.

The fire truck drove up, and Joey showed the firemen the

pond. When everything was ready, the boys dipped their torches in gasoline and lit them. While the men watched from a distance, Joey set fire to the corral and tossed torches into the sheds. Steve lobbed two torches into the cabin. Then the two boys stood together as close to the fire as they could, shielding their eyes against the smoke. Walls fell in upon themselves and ancient boards crashed to the ground as the hot flames devoured the last vestiges of Skeeter Hawkins. The boys' faces smarted from the heat of the fire, and tears streaked their sooty cheeks. Physical discomfort seemed a balm for their anguish. Once the flames died down, the firemen poked through the embers putting out flickers of flame with extinguishers. The sight of strangers walking around even the ashes of the property was so unpleasant that Joey and Steve were glad Skeeter had allowed them to burn the buildings.

"Let's get out of here!" Steve said quietly.

The boys drove out of the clearing in their trucks, honking good-bye to each other as they turned to go in their separate directions. Joey started to head home, then changed his mind and drove to the Oaks Cemetery. He parked the truck and got out, determined that this would be his last visit; he was not going to drive over every day until the mongrel died.

As Joey approached, Orval Faubus opened one eye and let out a sigh of disdain. None of his food had been touched, but Joey pulled out a packet of dry dog food and tore off the top. As he dropped three nuggets under the dog's nose, Orval Faubus snarled and grabbed his wrist. Joey threw off the dog, stood up, and announced, "You are the sorriest, meanest, dirtiest, dumbest, stubbornest, ugliest, hatefulest excuse for a dog that ever lived! Go ahead and die, you stupid jerk! You don't know how to act when people are nice!"

"Well then?" Joey heard Skeeter say.

"All right, Orval Faubus," Joey said calmly. Then he yelled, "Orval Faubus! Get up and get your backside out of this cemetery! We're going home! Let's go!" Joey slapped the dog on his haunch and took off toward the truck. As he opened the door a flash of dirty white jumped past him and landed on the seat.

"You stupid dog!" Joey said, jerking Orval Faubus back and forth in a vigorous show of affection. "You stupid old dog!" Joey climbed into the cab beside his partner and drove down the cemetery road whistling a now familiar tune.